REBIRTH

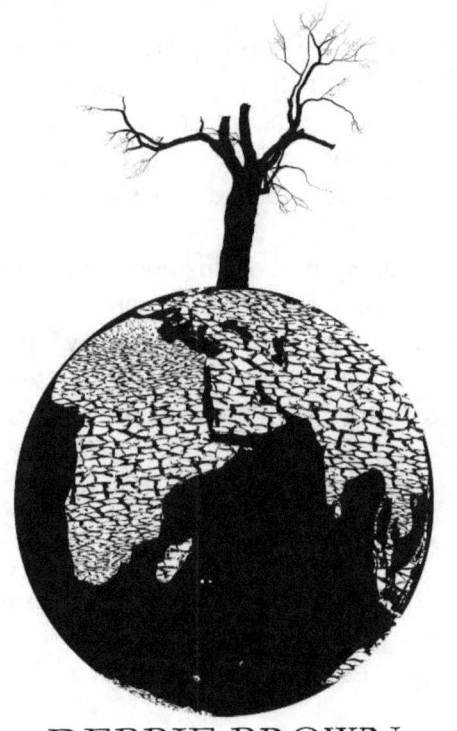

DEBBIE BROWN

REBIRTH
By
Debbie Brown
Copyright © Debbie Brown 2014
Cover Illustration by Ravenswood Publishing
Published by Mythos Press
(An Imprint of Ravenswood Publishing)

GMTA Publishing Group
6296 Philippi Church Rd.
Raeford, NC 28376
http://www.gmtapublishing.com

Printed in the U.S.A.

ISBN-13: 978-0615739861
ISBN-10: 0615739865

Dedication

Many thanks to my dear friends Kim and Ursula, to my family, and to my beloved writing instructor, Clara Gillow Clark. A special thanks to Kitty Bullard, I am so grateful to have met you.

Table of Contents

Chapter One

My head pounded from the pain. It was so bad I wanted to scream, but I knew if I did, *they* would hear me…and the last thing I wanted was for them to find me. I didn't even know who *they* were. A sob wracked my chest as the memory of the screams meshed with images of people being attacked amidst the falling buildings came back.

I still didn't understand what was going on and it didn't help that I couldn't see a thing. I felt cold, so cold. Darkness mixed with the eerie silence and memories of the cries for help…until nothing made sense anymore…until my mind slipped off into the oblivion of unconsciousness.

A sharp stabbing at my ribs made it hard to breathe. Overwhelmed by the pain and dizziness, I thought I was going to throw up. Still pinned under what was left of the ice-cream and soda shop I'd been in, my body twisted in a painful position, I had to accept there was nothing I could do about it. My last attempt to free myself had knocked something loose, which had hit me on the side of the head.

Footsteps! My heart raced, increasing the pounding in my head. Now I really felt like throwing up. *I hope they haven't found me. Maybe they won't notice me. Maybe I'll die under this pile of rubble…and to think my parents sent me here to be safe. Maybe it had all been planned. No, no, they wouldn't have done that. I don't want to die, but I can't even pull an arm free or move my legs. I don't even know if I'm visible. Maybe I'm paralyzed. Hard to focus…*

"Over here!" a young voice called out, startling me.

"Would you shut up!" an older voice snapped. "They're gonna hear you."

"Look," the first voice whispered.

Except for the wicked pounding in my head to the beat of my

out-of-control heart rate, I heard nothing. Were they still there? I had never been so scared in all my life. I felt someone touch my foot and my breath caught.

"Where's his head?" the older voice whispered. "I only see a foot. There's no way he's still alive with all this stuff on him, Jamie. "

No! No! No! Don't leave me here. I'm alive! I tried, but I couldn't make a sound.

"He's alive, Mitch. I can see it." The first voice was tinged with frustration. "His head's in here. I can see some hair."

Mitch sighed heavily. "I don't want to stick my hand in there. What if he's all gross?"

"I'll do it," Jamie said.

I could feel his fingers on my neck. What if they can't find a pulse and leave me here?

"Do you even know what you're doing?" Mitch asked impatiently, letting out another sigh. "Let me do it."

The small hand pulled back.

"Gross, there's blood on my hand," Jamie exclaimed.

"Shh!" Mitch admonished. "Do you want them to find all of us?"

"No," Jamie whispered. You could hear the fear in his voice.

Strong fingers moved to my neck this time. *I hope Mitch knows what he's doing. He's close enough to feel a pulse. Come on...yes! He found it.* Relief washed through me in soothing waves. *Now if only they could get me out.*

"Ok, he's alive. You were right," Mitch admitted.

"How are we going to get him out of here?" Jamie asked. "He looks like he's really stuck."

"Yeah, and he's hurt too. We have to try."

After what seemed like forever, the crushing weight that had been holding me in place was gone. I tried to fill my lungs with the first deep breath in hours, but another sharp stab of pain hit me. I heard myself moan. The acrid smell of smoke penetrated my dust filled nose.

"It's OK," Jamie's voice whispered in my ear. "You're almost out."

"See if you can find some water and a cloth to wipe the blood from his face," Mitch said to Jamie in a hushed voice. "What's your name?" he said to me as he removed the last of the debris from my body.

My mouth was so dry I couldn't speak. I tried pushing myself up but my breath caught as another wave of pain hit. My eyelids were glued shut. Gingerly I raised a hand to my face. I could feel the sticky blood across my forehead and cheek.

"Don't try and move just yet. My little brother is looking for some water or something." He left a hand on my shoulder.

The crunching sound told me Jamie was moving closer. "I found bottled water, a hand towel and a straw so he can drink lying down," he whispered to his brother.

"Good job."

I heard the top being twisted off the bottle and then felt a tap on my shoulder. "Try and take a sip," Mitch said as he gently placed the straw to my lips. "Hold the bottle of water, Jamie. I'm gonna try and clean up his face a bit."

I hadn't realized just how thirsty I was. I greedily drank until my stomach cramped. Catching my breath I tried to clear my throat. "Thanks," I managed to croak out.

"Shh!" Jamie hushed me. In any other circumstance, it would have been funny.

"Let me know if I hurt you." Mitch wiped my cheek and eye with a damp cloth that smelled of soured milk. He rubbed a little harder. "There's a lot of blood."

Stiffly, I managed to prop myself up on the debris-covered floor. "Help me so I can sit." A burst of pain shot through my leg. I clenched my teeth and sat up. "Give me the cloth and water." I held out my hands and felt the damp rag and bottle being pushed into them. Placing the smelly cloth on my leg I lifted the bottle to my forehead and poured some water over my eyelid, rubbing the blood from my eyelashes. A bit of light became visible through one eye as I managed to pry it open slightly. The metallic smell of my blood filled my nose, turning my stomach. I'd never make a good doctor like Mom. She never seemed to mind the blood or the mess.

Dropping the water as a wave of dizziness hit, I struggled against the overwhelming urge to vomit. Moaning as my mind ran through all sorts of scenarios, I prayed it wasn't because of a severe head injury. I had seen a man die in Kosovo after a blow to the head.

As the bright spots that danced before my eyes subsided, I realized that I was being supported by both boys. Jamie's voice was filled with concern. "Is he going to be OK?"

"I'm fine," I managed to say. "Could I have another sip of water?" With one eyelid open I took my first look at my rescuers. Mitch looked about fourteen, maybe fifteen, blonde hair, hazel eyes, and he was built like a football player. Jamie couldn't have been more than seven, with light blue eyes, white-blonde hair and a delicate build. Judging by the bluish tinge to his lips, he was probably asthmatic. Jamie watched as I took another sip. "Do you guys want any water?"

Jamie nodded. Mitch studied me as he twisted the cap off another bottle for his brother. A look of recognition crossed his face. "Aren't you that new kid who just transferred to our school?"

I nodded as I pulled the last clump of dried blood, along with a few black eyelashes, from my lid. Both eyes were open now. "My name is Aleksei. Are we in the same level?"

"No, I think you're a grade higher. I don't think there's a student in our school who doesn't know about you."

I frowned. "Know what exactly?" I passed my hands over my body, checking for injuries. The cut on my left temple continued to bleed.

"You know, that you'd never gone to school before and that you grew up in the jungle," Mitch admitted.

"Yeah, with wild animals," exclaimed Jamie.

I choked on my sip of water. "I think you're confusing me with Tarzan or Mogli." I lifted my shirt to get a look at my ribs. They were a mottled mass of pink, blue and purple, but I didn't think any were broken. I couldn't pull my pant leg up enough to see how bad my thigh was, but the bleeding had stopped and I could move it. OK, no broken bones but I felt bruised from head to toe.

"Do you know who those guys were?" Mitch asked. The expression on his face was unreadable and his voice dropped to almost a whisper. "*What* they were?" He shot a glance at Jamie who was quietly sipping his water.

I shook my throbbing head slowly. "It all happened so fast." The sounds of the screams came back to me. I saw people running frantically through the streets, falling as if hit with some kind of taser, and then vanishing. The dark-blue clad attackers were built like tall, muscular men. Their faces were not visible behind the mirror-like visors of their helmets. "How bad is it out there?"

Mitch shook his head. "Almost everything has been damaged and some buildings were completely destroyed." I looked around at the demolished ice cream shop. The front of the store was now a gaping hole. The three-story building it had been attached to was nothing but a smoldering pile of rubble. Black columns of smoke rose from various buildings throughout the city and in the fading daylight I could see fires burning. It looked more like a war zone than rural Montana. The smell didn't remind me of war, it was different this time. There was the smell of smoke, burnt wood and plastic, but there was something missing and I couldn't quite figure it out. I realized the air didn't smell of gunpowder or explosives, and the smell of carnage was also absent, but that was hopefully a good sign. Dust particles still hovered in the air.

A scream caught our attention. The hair on my arms stood on end as I heard shouts and cries coming from outside. *They* must be back. "Come on," I whispered to Mitch and Jamie. "We've got to hide." My heart pounded in my ears, bringing my headache back with a vengeance. "Let's get behind the counter, maybe we can hide in the back room or something." Then I remembered the trap door in the floor leading to the basement. "Follow me."

I had seen the owner coming out of it this morning when I had come to ask for a job. My aunt, with whom I had been staying with since my arrival less than two weeks ago, had insisted. She said that at fifteen, I had to have a part-time job. I guess she didn't want me to be more of a burden than necessary.

"Climb down," I said. I handed Mitch a flashlight from the bottom shelf of the counter that the trap door was behind. "I'm gonna grab a few things from the office and be down in a minute."

"Come on, Jamie." Mitch helped his little brother down the rickety, ladder-like steps. "We'll be safe in here." He shot me a glance, almost pleading that it be the truth. It was a look I had seen often over the years, working alongside my parents.

I limped to the back room, grabbed the first aid kit and a reusable shopping bag. I proceeded to fill it with bottles of juice, water and stuff to make sandwiches. With no power it wouldn't take long for food to go bad, and then things were really going to smell.

Another scream pierced the air, louder this time. "Here, grab the bag," I said to Mitch as I climbed down into the basement on shaky legs. The room smelled dank and dusty. Not much good if Jamie was asthmatic. I could barely make out the shelves that lined the wall. An old wooden table and two chairs were at the far end of the small room, and a cot with wool blankets stuck out from behind the stairs.

"This place is creepy," Jamie said with a cough. "I wonder what Mr. Peterson used it for."

I could hear him start to wheeze. Damn. "Do you have your inhaler with you?" I asked.

Mitch whirled around. "How'd you know?"

I shrugged. "Mom's a doctor. I've seen all kinds of things." I turned my attention back to Jamie. "So?"

He checked his pockets then his eyes widened as he shook his head. "I must have lost it."

I let out a breath. "OK. I'm going back up for a few things. I'll be right back." My mind ran through possible substitutes for bronchodilators. I stopped short just as I was about to lift the door up. Footsteps! They were in the store!

Mitch held his brother close and shut the light. I didn't dare move. The throbbing in my leg matched the pounding of my head as I stood still on the old, wooden excuse for stairs. My hands burned from holding the top of the ladder so tight. I was breathing through my mouth now, trying not to make a sound. I could hear Jamie whimper and Mitch comfort him. Dust fell through the edge of the trap door and slid over my arms as someone stomped around what was left of the shop. They were right over my head. A loud crash and a thud filled the air. I held my breath, not daring to move. Jamie's wheezing was getting louder. Muffled cries, then the stomping of their boots led me to believe they were gone. A cold droplet of sweat trickled down my back.

I waited until I thought my legs would give out. Gathering my courage, I pushed on the door to take a peek. It wouldn't budge. No! They must have knocked something onto it. I took a step up the ladder so I could brace my shoulder against the door. Grunting, I pushed with all my might. We were trapped!

I jumped when Mitch climbed up behind me. "Let me help," he whispered. I stepped down shakily so he could get in close.

The sound of something sliding off the door, followed by a crash resounded throughout the small basement. Everyone held their breath, waiting for the footsteps to return. Nothing. Mitch stepped down and let me climb back up. I felt light headed as I lifted the door up enough to look out. It was dark now, but everything was quiet and gave me no reason to believe *they* were still here.

Taking a deep breath, I climbed up, careful not to make noise. It was so dark in the shop that I could barely make out the shadows that surrounded me. Using a flashlight was out of the question. The crunching sounds made by my steps seemed amplified in the dark, and I was afraid they could be heard throughout the street.

Moonlight appeared through a break in the clouds, giving me just enough light to see. *OK, I can do this*. I rummaged through the kitchen shelves looking for supplies. The packaging used here was unfamiliar to me and I had to open everything. Prying the lid off a tin I took a whiff of the contents. Finally, just what I needed.

I scurried back to the door and handed Mitch my findings. He snapped on the flashlight as I shut the trap door behind myself. I took a moment to gather my thoughts as he went back to comfort his brother. The wheezing wasn't letting up, but then I didn't expect it to under the circumstances. Jamie needed to get out of the damp, dusty basement. Stress alone could trigger an attack and he didn't need anything to add to it.

I rummaged through the basement supplies, looking for anything we might be able to use. Under the cot behind the steps was a wooden box, like an old army footlocker. Inside, I found a butane camp stove, two compact camping pots, an old percolator, a lantern and some other potentially useful items. "Do you know how to light this?" I held up the lantern to Mitch.

"Sure, give it here. Looks just like the one my grandpa has." He took it and set it on the table, explaining to Jamie how to light it. Good, that'll keep his mind busy.

I took out the stove and percolator, closed the lid on the wooden box and pulled it away from the bed to use as a table. "Hand me a bottle of water." I poured the contents of the plastic bottle into the tin percolator and threw a handful of coffee into the basket. This, I was used to.

"Is that what you went out there for?" Mitch's voice growled. "A cup of coffee?"

"It's for your brother."

"What the heck's wrong with you?" His voice was getting louder.

I held up a hand. "Coffee's a natural bronchodilator." I pulled him closer. "We need to get him settled before he has a full blown attack." I clenched my jaw. "We need to regroup and formulate a plan."

"What are you talking about?" Mitch was obviously losing patience.

I turned to Mitch, pressing my lips as I thought. "We can't stay here. The damp, dusty environment isn't good for your brother. We have to get away from the city and find shelter." I leaned in closer and lowered my voice. "We don't know if *they* are still around, or if they'll come back."

He sat on the edge of the cot and passed a hand over his face. He looked tired and worn.

"I'm hungry," Jamie said in a whiny voice. Mitch just looked at me.

I poured some of the strong, dark coffee into the small pot and stood. "We'll let this cool a bit," I said to Mitch. Turning to Jamie I pointed to the cot. "Why don't you settle down here while Mitch and I make you something to eat?"

Jamie's eyes found his brother's. "Come on Squirt, I'll make you something special."

Sliding off the chair Jamie made his way to the cot, dragging his feet. He muttered something under his breath as he plopped down onto the cot.

Mitch leaned in closer. "What'd you say?" His tone was abrupt.

"Your food stinks." Jamie lifted his head to look at his brother.

I felt the side of my mouth curl into a smile. "Well then you're lucky. I can cook anything," I reassured him.

"Yeah, like rat on a stick," Mitch said to Jamie sarcastically.

OK, so Mitch was a little testy. I didn't bother telling them that I had actually seen that 'delicacy', though I had passed on trying it.

After eating, Jamie fell asleep on the cot, exhausted. His breathing was better after a few sips of coffee, much to his brother's surprise.

Mitch, sitting across from me at the little wooden table, sipped from a bottle of juice. "What do we do now?" His eyes searched my face.

I looked around the small dingy room, barely lit by the camp light. "We can't stay here."

Mitch shook his head. "I'm not sure I'm ready to go back out there." A flash of something unreadable crossed his face.

"Did you see them?"

He nodded slowly. "I have never seen anyone that looked like that before. It's not like they came from another country or something." He shuddered.

A knot formed in the pit of my stomach. That was the impression I had had as well. *They* were some kind of hostile attackers or invaders. I couldn't bring myself to consider them being, well, alien.

"What do you think they did with everyone?" Mitch's question brought me back to the basement.

I had seen people drop to the ground and literally vanish. I let out a sigh. "If we were playing a game, answering anything off the top of our heads, I'd be inclined to say they were killed or captured by the invaders." I felt an icy chill creep up my spine.

Mitch dropped his head and stared at the floor. "If I hadn't seen it with my own eyes…" his voice trailed off. He grabbed the sides of his head with his hands and propped his elbows on his knees.

"How come you didn't get caught by them?" I waited for him to raise his head and look at me.

He shook his head. "I don't know. When they stormed the streets and people started dropping like flies, I was with Jamie on the playground. Once people began to realize what was going on, they started running and screaming." He looked over at his sleeping brother. "I grabbed him and hid in the filter room under the public pool. I have never been so scared in all my life."

I considered Mitch's words. I had been in dangerous situations before, but somehow it wasn't the same this time. I had no idea what we were up against, and I didn't have my parents or the relief community guiding our steps.

Chapter Two

The slow and rhythmic breathing coming from both Mitch and Jamie were the only sounds I could hear as I lay shivering in the dark. At least they seemed to be able to sleep. I reached over my head to where the flashlight lay on the floor. My whole body screamed in protest to my movement, but then, I was in pain no matter what. Flicking on the light I sat up and shone it onto Mitch's watch. It should be daylight by now.

Mitch bolted upright and I placed a hand on his shoulder. "It's OK. I'm just going to take a peek topside."

He nodded, grunting as he wiped his eyes. "See if you can find us something to eat," he whispered in a hoarse voice.

In an attempt to ease the tension in my body, I leaned forward and stretched. I cautiously made my way up the steps to the trap door, taking a moment to listen for any outside activity. Nothing. Taking a deep breath, and gathering my courage, I braced my shoulder against the dirty door and lifted it an inch. Daylight streamed in through the crack. Swallowing the lump forming in my throat, I lifted the door and climbed out into the eerie silence.

Rooted in place I turned to look outside. A few columns of smoke still rose in the distance. My skin crawled. Something just wasn't right. I stood there, in total silence, when I should have been surrounded by the sounds of rescue crews, police and firemen, helicopters…

"You coming?" Mitch whispered from below.

I jumped as though he had yelled it out. My legs went weak but I shook it off. "Give me a minute." Remembering my task, I hurried to collect what could be salvaged for breakfast. I paused on the steps of the ladder before closing myself in and listened again. There were no signs of life. No people, no animals, no insects…nothing but silence. I closed the door over my head and jumped down to face Mitch, shutting out the lifelessness above.

"Jamie's still asleep." Mitch glanced back at his brother on the cot as he spread the food on the table. "What's the plan?"

I took a long breath and sat on one of the wooden chairs. "We need to find shelter away from the city." I tried to come up with a plan of action.

"I agree," Mitch said. "My gut's screaming for us to get out of here too, but..." he hesitated. His eyes met mine. "I'm terrified." He held my stare.

"So am I," I admitted. "At least we've got each other. Maybe we'll find others."

Mitch sniffed the piece of meat he was holding. "You sure this is safe?"

I nodded. "I shoved stuff in the freezer last night, knowing things would be going bad fast once the sun came out." It had been very hot in the city yesterday and the forecast was calling for more of the same for today.

"It's not frozen, but it is cool and doesn't smell bad." Mitch divided the food up into three piles. He tilted his head to the side. "Did you notice how quiet it is out there?" He shuddered.

"Yeah." I grabbed a juice bottle and twisted off the cap. Downing half in one sip, I tried not to think for a minute.

Mitch continued, "I saw the television reports after the earthquake in Haiti. There was screaming, rioting and all kinds of action." He took a bottle of juice for himself and put out another for the still sleeping Jamie. Wiping his mouth with the back of his sleeve, he shifted in his chair and leaned in close to me. "Do you think everyone's been taken?" His voice dropped to a whisper, "Or killed?" His eyes darted back to his brother.

I shook my head slowly. What did I think happened? "I don't want to stay around here to find out. If there are bodies in the rubble, and I don't see how there couldn't be, things are going to get vile-smelling."

"Shit. I didn't think about that." Mitch jumped up, knocking his chair over and startling Jamie.

Sitting up on the cot, Jamie scrubbed sleep from his eyes. "About what?" He swung his scrawny legs over the edge of the cot and sat up, instantly overcome by a coughing fit.

I scooted from the chair and went to Jamie. Taking his hands, I began speaking slowly to him. "Look at me." I bent to catch his gaze. "Breathe with me, slowly." His eyes were wide with panic but he nodded. "That's it, good. Breathe with me." I wiped the tears from his cheeks, keeping a respiratory rhythm he could match. Smiling with relief, I drew him into a hug. I could see Mitch's face over Jamie's shoulder; all the color seemed to have drained from it. I mouthed the word *coffee* to Mitch, and once it registered, he got up to get Jamie a cup.

We ate in silence as I mulled through our options. Not knowing the scope of the damage weighed heavily on me. Was it local, national or on a planetary level? Were we the only ones left? I found that hard to believe, but then, where were the rescue crews? A glance over in Mitch's direction told me he was lost in his own thoughts.

Jamie was the first to speak. "Can we go now?" He looked around the room with his sunken eyes. "I don't like it here."

"Eat something first," Mitch said, pointing to the food on the table.

I stood and paced around the room. I had no idea what to do. I really believed we needed to get away from here. A clipboard left on a dusty shelf caught my attention. Flipping the papers over, I used the attached ballpoint pen to scribble a list of supplies. We needed food, for sure, a first aid kit with an inhaler for Jamie, tools, bedding, shelter and transportation. I doodled on the page and wondered if my parents were still alive. I exhaled sharply out of frustration. I had been sent here, supposedly for my own safety. They promised to come for me once they'd relocated to the next country. Who'd have thought I'd be in danger in Montana?

"Alex," Mitch's voice intruded on my thoughts.

"Aleksei," I corrected.

The look on his face said he really didn't care. "Are we going or not?" His eyes darted around the room. "I'm not too crazy about this place myself."

"Let's do it. We can't stay here forever." I was trying hard to convince myself of that, but the thought of stepping out into this kind of unknown was terrifying. "I'll go first. Wait for my signal." Daylight poured into the depths of our shelter as I lifted the trap door. My skin crawled as I climbed out and took my first good look at the city. Although some buildings had been hit less than others, there were still no signs of life anywhere. "Come on up," I said in a hushed voice. I hoped this wasn't a mistake.

"I need to get a better look at this," Mitch said from behind me.

"What are you going to do?" Jamie asked, leaning heavily on his brother.

Mitch looked down at his little brother and rested a hand on his shoulder. "You help Aleksei get supplies, and I'm going to run up to the top of that building and take a look around." He pointed across the street to an apartment building that had two sides and a fire escape still intact. "Stay here where it's safe, just give me a couple of minutes to check things out." He handed me the clipboard I had left behind. "I'll see if I can figure out which way we should go."

I nodded and guided Jamie behind the counter. "Let's sit here a minute, OK? I need your help with the list." I followed Mitch's progress from my spot on the floor, careful to keep Jamie's attention from his brother. "What do you think we need?"

"Why can't we just go home?" He frowned. "I don't like this." He let out a breath of exasperation.

I forced a smile and readjusted my leg. My whole body felt as though it had been through the wringer. "I don't care for it much myself." I held up the pen and pointed to the clipboard. "Let's make our list and see if we can get out of here." I spotted my backpack on the counter, just where I had left it. Blowing the layer of dust off it, and away from Jamie, I pushed my notebook and pencil case aside and filled it with water and juice bottles. I grabbed what was left of the cold cuts I had placed in the freezer the night before, took some bread and cheese and shoved it all into my pack, along with a sharp knife. We might need it for more than just sandwiches.

"Cookies," Jamie blurted out.

"You want cookies." OK, I can humour him. I jotted down the item and added a few *essential* items of my own. I tried to remember the seven enemies of survival. Cold or heat, so temperature, pain, fear, hunger, thirst, shelter and what was that last one...

"Chocolate." Jamie continued with his list.

I looked at him and suppressed a smile. "That's a good one." Mitch had made it to the top of the building and stood against the cloudless sky. I watched as he turned slowly, taking in the situation. I saw him stiffen and lean forward, as if he were trying to get a better view. He dropped down out of sight and I saw his feet appear over the edge of the building. He slid down the stairs faster than if he'd have jumped. Shit. "Stay here, Jamie, I'll be right back."

I met Mitch at the gaping hole in the building. His face was flushed and he was breathing heavily. "We've got to get out of here now." He spoke in a low voice, but the urgency made my skin crawl.

"Lead the way." I had learned from living in dangerous areas that questions could wait, and that when the signal was given to evacuate, nothing else mattered.

He pointed to the back of the store, still gasping to catch his breath. "Jamie, time to leave," he ordered.

Scrambling to his feet Jamie was ushered out the back door before he could turn around. I followed Mitch through the park behind the building and up the hill. Jamie fared better outside. Good.

At the top of the hill Jamie ran to the public washrooms. It probably didn't matter if they were non-functional. I stopped Mitch from following his brother in so I could get some answers. "What did you see?"

"I don't know what I saw," he snapped. "There's this orange powder falling from the sky, and I swear it's melting or dissolving buildings and debris down to the ground. Somehow the trees don't seem to be affected, but I want to be as far away as I can get from here when the orange stuff reaches this part of town." He went in after Jamie.

I had no idea how fast this was happening, but I was pretty sure we wouldn't get far enough on foot to be safe. I had seen hopelessness in the countries my parents had worked in over the years, but this was the first time I actually felt it.

Mitch came out with his brother. "If you need to go, do it. You get one flush."

Walking down the hill we passed by a Jeep dealership. "Hurry!" I ran to the unlocked door and into the offices rummaging through drawers and shelves.

"What are you looking for?" Mitch asked as he caught up to me.

"Help me find the keys. We'll get out of here faster if we can use one of the Jeeps." On a bulletin board I found a series of keys and quickly pulled them off.

"Sure, if one of us knew how to drive!"

I shrugged off his comment. "I know how. I've been in countries where the only requirement was to be able to reach the pedals. Come on."

We unlocked a Jeep Commander and I got in behind the wheel and froze.

Mitch was watching me. "Now what? I thought you said you could drive." His patience was obviously not improving.

I held up a hand as I looked over the controls. "The vehicle I learned on had its steering column on your side." I put the key into the ignition and turned the key without starting the engine. Damn, we weren't going to go far on a quarter tank of gas. I pressed my lips together. "OK, we're going to have to run back to the garage and get a syphon or some tubing. We need to siphon gas." I looked around at the other vehicles. Two demonstrator models were equipped with extra gas cans, attached to the rear door. Good, we'd take those too.

We found out it was impossible to siphon gas from a new car so we used the older employee vehicles. After almost swallowing a mouthful of gasoline, we were able to fill the gas cans along with the Jeep's tank. I had no idea how far it could take us, but I figured we could always siphon other vehicles along the way.

Jamie sat on the backseat, dozing as we pulled out of the dealership. Mitch wiped a hand over his eyes then grimaced as he smelled his fingers. "I could use a shower," he said glumly.

"Let's see if we can grab some stuff from any stores that might still be standing." We were going to need all the help we could get if we were going to survive. I let my mind wander from the road for only a second, but it was a second more than I should have.

"Watch out!" Mitch grabbed the dash and door as I swerved away from a pile of debris strewn across the street. The passenger side climbed up onto the debris and shook them violently before the jeep came to a stop.

Wiping the sweat from my eyes with my sleeve, I gripped the steering wheel with a shaky hand as I slowly maneuvered the jeep around the pile and back onto the street.

"Stop!" Jamie pulled on the back of my seat.

"Now what?" I asked, a little frustrated.

"Let me out, I have to help her." Jamie was becoming frantic and started wheezing again.

"Calm down." Mitch turned to his brother and his gaze followed Jamie's outstretched arm. "Hold on a minute," he said to me. He pointed to someone frantically pulling debris from the side of a house. "I'll go." He stepped out of the Jeep and jogged toward the figure.

Jamie struggled to climb into the front seat. "It's a girl," he exclaimed. Both Mitch and the girl were talking, waving their hands in the air in an animated discussion. Mitch pointed to the Jeep repeatedly, only to get a firm 'no' and shake of her head. She was a full head shorter than Mitch, and couldn't have weighed more than ninety pounds. Her wavy, dark brown hair bobbed up and down as she argued with him. I let out a sigh. "Stay put, will you?" I said to Jamie. "I think Mitch could use a hand." I jumped down from the jeep and hurried to the pair, my body protesting loudly. It really wasn't the time to be arguing.

"I'm not leaving without her!" the girl was trying to clear a path into the remains of the house. She wiped her dirty hands on her equally dirty, tight-fitting jeans.

Mitch turned to me, his face constricted with frustration. "She thinks her dog is still in there, alive." He pointed toward the crumbled home.

My heart sank. We needed to get out of here, now, but the thought of leaving a dog behind was unbearable. During one of the raids on the village where my parents had been lending aid, hurt and scared animals had been abandoned and left to die. I had cried for days. Without saying a word, I dropped down next to the girl and started pulling stuff out of the way. I was already stiff and sore, and it seemed as though my body was destined for non-stop abuse.

Mitch growled, again, but then he joined us in our attempts. "Are you sure he's in there?" He didn't stop to look at her.

Jamie, ignoring the order to stay put appeared beside us. "There's nobody in there."

The girl shot Jamie a nasty look but turned her attention back to the broken end of the dog's leash she'd just uncovered. It looked as though the dog took cover after the house came down. She started tugging on it.

"Don't you think he'd be barking if he was still alive?" Mitch suggested roughly.

She turned on him. "She! And I'm not leaving without her." The girl dropped to her knees, trying to peer inside. She reached her arm in and tugged at the leash. This time it came free and she pulled it out of the house. The collar was empty.

I looked at Mitch and closed my eyes, shaking my head. "We should get out of here."

The girl dropped her head and stuffed the pink collar into her pocket.

"What's your name?" Mitch asked as he herded Jamie back to the Jeep.

"Krisztina," she answered as she followed us back to the Jeep. Without another word she climbed into the backseat next to Jamie.

"There's no one in there," was all Jamie said.

Continuing on our way, we stared silently at the destruction that surrounded us. In the rear-view mirror, I could see Jamie watching Krisztina. I smiled to myself. Last night he had been upfront and chatty, but I guess her demeanor held him off.

Mitch pointed off to the right. "Stop here."

I followed his outstretched arm to what was left of a Wal-Mart store. We could probably find some useful items here. Climbing over the sidewalk to avoid fallen debris, I eased the jeep close to the building where the McDonald's plate-glass window had been, the perfect entrance. I just hoped the section still standing wasn't clothing. We needed food and camping material.

Once inside, we decided to split up and collect what we thought we could use. Then meet back after about fifteen minutes. Mitch turned back to Jamie. "You coming with me?"

Jamie shook his head, avoiding Mitch's eyes. "I want to go with Aleksei."

Mitch shrugged and headed off in his assigned direction. Krisztina went off for food and I headed to the pharmacy. First things on the list were an inhaler and a first-aid kit. After grabbing what I thought was essential, I looked for the camping section. Daylight from the open storefront didn't reach far enough back to let me find what I needed. Fortunately, flashlights were abundant. A tent, butane stove, pots, fire stone, sleeping bags, folding chairs…I wished I would have taken a minivan. Oh well, we'd grab what we could. The sound of Jamie talking to someone startled me. I whirled around to face him and asked in a hushed voice, "Who are you talking to?" My eyes followed the direction in which he was pointing. My blood ran cold as I prayed it wasn't one of those blue-clad invaders.

"Her," he answered as though there was nothing out of the norm.

My flashlight beam scanned the area. There was nothing there. The hair on my arms stood on end as I crouched down next to him. "I don't see anyone."

He let out a dramatic sigh and took the flashlight from me, redirecting the light. "Her," he said with emphasis.

"Could you help me find my baby brother?" She didn't wait for an answer; she just turned and crawled through a pile of fallen debris.

Grabbing a flashlight Jamie scurried after her, forcing his way through the debris behind her. Great.

"Where'd Jamie go?" Mitch's voice came up behind me.

Startled, I jumped back, holding my chest. "Give me a little warning next time."

"Mitch! Come help us," Jamie called from the other side of the rubble.

In a few strides he crossed the floor to Jamie's voice. "You get out of there this minute!" He passed a hand through his hair nervously. "Did you hear me?"

"Not 'till we find J.J.," came a little voice.

Mitch's head snapped to meet my gaze.

I shrugged. "She was just standing there. Jamie went in after her."

"Come on, Mitch! We need your help." He poked his head through the crawl space.

I thought Mitch was going to lose it. He grabbed Jamie by the shoulders and pulled his brother out. "Don't you ever do that again!"

Jamie blinked. "But I was helping Ally find her baby brother."

Mitch dropped down to look into the opening with his flashlight. "Ally! You come out here. It's not safe."

"No, I have to find J.J.," came the little voice.

Mitch's face turned red. He started pulling debris away from the door and tossing it every which way. Jamie hid behind my legs just as Krisztina joined me to watch. I wasn't even sure if it would be wise to help with him recklessly tossing stuff around.

Pausing to stretch his back, Mitch turned back to us. "Jamie, can you get her out?"

Jamie peeked around from behind my legs and shook his head. "She wants to find her baby brother."

Mitch dropped down onto one knee, wiping the sweat from his forehead with the back of his sleeve. "Look, we have *got* to get out of here. It's not safe." He looked around, obviously trying to think of something. "If there was a baby, he'd be crying."

Again, Jamie shook his head. "He's there. He's just sleeping."

Mitch looked up at me and I shrugged. "He's been right all along." I moved in to help.

After about forty minutes of continuous effort, we managed to clear enough of the material away to get in to where Ally had gone. Mitch stopped dead as the beam of his flashlight came to rest on Ally's small form. She was sitting under a table, cradling a sleeping baby.

"We're going to need diapers," I said.

Chapter Three

I grunted as I slammed the jeep door closed. I had visions of the whole thing popping open and spewing its entire contents across the road. Good thing Mitch found that extra rooftop storage for the Jeep. We even had a few bags hanging out the back window. I still had no idea as to the city's rate of destruction and couldn't risk leaving behind essential items.

"Where are we going?" Krisztina asked. It was the first time she'd spoken since she'd left her house.

I looked at Mitch. "Anywhere, as long as it's far away from the city."

"Well now that's a plan," she barked back.

Mitch, not wearing a seatbelt, turned to face her. "What's your plan? Why don't you tell us where we should go, or what we should do?"

Ally pointed to the built in GPS. "Why don't you ask the lady? Mommy always did when she didn't know where she was going."

Mitch shot me a glance and I shrugged. He started poking at the buttons but nothing happened.

"You have to stop or it won't work," Ally added. "Mommy's tried."

I pulled over to the side and put the jeep in park. This time the screen came to life, showing a map of the area. "That's good enough," I said. "It's not like we need directions to the local tourist attractions." Then I remembered the list my father had given me before I'd been sent here. There were supposedly caves with hot springs in the area. They could act as a natural shelter and heat source. I wasn't too sure how Jamie's lungs would handle it, but I had to figure something out.

As we drove away from the city and into the wooded areas the destruction became less evident. Even the roads were intact. If not for the occasional abandoned car, we could have convinced ourselves that everything was fine.

J.J. chose that moment to wake up and let out a wail, breaking the solemn silence in the car. Mitch turned to Krisztina. "Aren't you going to handle it?"

In the rear view mirror I caught the look of fury she flashed Mitch. "You think that because I'm a girl, that because—" She made some crude reference to her anatomy then crossed her arms across her chest and turned to look out the window.

Ally, without a word reached for the diaper bag and pulled out a pacifier. Jamie produced the bottle of formula he'd been holding between his legs since they'd left the crumbled store and J.J. reached for it hungrily. The cries instantly subsided as the pressing need was met.

An hour into our drive everyone had fallen asleep. Left alone with my thoughts as I drove down the road, I couldn't help but wonder if my parents had vanished as well, or if they even knew of the disaster that had struck us here. I wondered if they would be more worried about me than any of the other victims. Somehow I couldn't convince myself that they would. My gaze went to each of the sleeping faces and I felt the heavy weight of responsibility settle onto my shoulders. I needed to be reassured and protected just as much as the others, but yet again it seemed as though everyone else's needs would come first.

Bringing the Jeep to a stop near the hot springs, my eyes settled on the rear-view mirror, giving me a clear view of my reflection. It was the first time I saw the bruises that covered my tanned face. My deep blue eyes looked like my father's with their newly formed stress lines and fatigue showing. A layer of dust coated my wavy black hair and the gash near my temple had caked blood around the poorly taped bandage. I'd tend to my needs later.

With a sigh of exhaustion, I steered the Jeep onto the dirt road that led to the edge of the cliffs and the hot spring outlet. Even here, I had yet to see a bird or animal. At least we wouldn't have to worry about being mauled by a bear.

Edging the Jeep closer to the cliffs, my attention was drawn to the strange rock formation. It looked like a huge slab of stone jutting out from the base of the cliff, offering a natural shelter. Maybe we could make something out of it. I parked some thirty yards from the formation, keeping the jeep close to the woods as I quietly slipped out of the vehicle and began unloading. They should be helping, I thought bitterly, but then they would be more helpful if they were rested.

Mitch wandered sleepily over to the tent I had just finished setting up. "Why didn't you wake me?" He stretched and yawned, turning to take in our surroundings.

I shrugged. "You needed to sleep." I handed him another tent, one that practically set itself up. "Set up over here and start putting our food and supplies into it. If we can make another run back into town while the store is still standing, we should load up."

Mitch nodded. "Good idea." He shuddered as he stepped away from the newly popped up tent. "All this silence is just creepy."

I nodded in agreement as I tossed the mats and sleeping bags into the tent I had set up. I had never seen such a thing. At 5'10", I could walk freely through it and it had an extra room at the back as well as rooms on the left and the right. The box said it housed thirteen people. I had seen entire families living in less than half this space, and to think one tent could have kept them dry and bug free.

I set up beds for the boys on the right and girls on the left. We could use the back section to change and wash. The main area could be our common room. I carried the baby supplies into the back room and almost tripped over Jamie. He was on his knees unrolling the sleeping bags onto the already laid out mats. I smiled at him and ruffled his hair. "Good job!"

He puffed his scrawny chest out and smiled. "Thanks."

"How are you feeling?" I asked as I looked him over. His color was good, and he didn't seem to be wheezing.

He gave a one-shoulder shrug and looked away. "Hungry."

I let out a soft chuckle. "You finish up with the bedding and I'll go heat up something to eat."

He nodded earnestly as he attacked the bedding.

Outside, I pulled out the butane stove and slipped in a canister. Unpacking the compact set of pots, I set them on the ground near the stove and reached for a few cans of stew. Frowning, I rummaged through the tools we had brought, looking for a can opener. Great, we'd have to add that to our list. I sat back on my heels and passed a hand through my dirty hair. I turned as a pungent smell met my nose. Ally was standing behind me holding a wiggling baby in her arms. "I think he needs a change." I reached out for him. "Go get what we need and I'll give you a hand."

She nodded and scurried back to the Jeep for the diaper bag. In her eagerness to return quickly, she tripped over a branch and landed spread-eagle on the ground. Mitch hurried over and scooped her up. He dusted off her jumper and looked into her face. "Are you OK?"

Wide-eyed and lower lip trembling, she nodded. "I'm sorry, I didn't mean to…" She shook her blonde head frantically.

"Hey, it's OK," Mitch reassured her. He looked over his shoulder at me and frowned. Turning back to Ally he brushed the curls away from her face. "Are you hurt?"

Tears welled in her eyes as she bit her lower lip. "I'm OK," she whispered. "I have to change J.J.'s diaper."

Jamie, who had come out of the tent as Ally fell, scooped the contents of the diaper bag up and stood waiting.

"The first-aid kit is in the back room of the tent," I said to Mitch in a low voice. Blood had appeared on Ally's scraped knees and elbow. I gave the brave six-year-old a reassuring look. "Jamie and I will tackle the diaper."

Jamie shook his head with force. "Nuh-huh, he sti–" His eyes widened at Mitch's glare. "I got the diaper bag," he offered and followed me into the tent.

Some thirty minutes later, Krisztina joined our group as we ladled out the warm stew. We had opened the cans using the opener in J.J.'s diaper bag, used for the formula tins. Mitch shot her a glance. "Nice of you to join us," he growled as he handed her a bowl. He turned back to the group and ignored her, not moving over to include her in our circle.

She sniffed it and wrinkled her nose. "Ugh, I am not eating this."

Mitch grabbed the bowl from her hands. "Fine, starve."

Her eyes narrowed, she crossed her arms and stomped off towards the cliffs.

I let out a long breath. "Would you come back here, please," I said through clenched teeth. "We need to get organized."

She spun around and cocked her head. "Look, I didn't ask to be here with you guys. I'm not into this whole communing with nature scene." She waved her hands to encompass the area.

"That's fine with me." I stood and handed my empty bowl to Mitch. "I was gonna leave her here to watch the kids while we went back to load up on more supplies, but I guess I'll drop her off at her house and you can hold the fort."

Her jaw dropped. "You can't just leave me there!"

I squared my shoulders and held her gaze. "None of us chose to be here. We have to make do as best we can. If you don't want to contribute, then fine, but you aren't staying here." I turned back to Mitch. "I'll be back as soon as I can. Do you think you can manage?"

He nodded.

"I'll help," Ally chimed in shyly. It seemed as though Mitch had a fan.

"Get in the Jeep," I nodded to Krisztina. I was too tired to argue, too angry to reason.

* * *

The sun had set by the time I made it back to the group. Krisztina hadn't said a word the whole time, but she had helped me load up the Jeep with anything and everything we could shove into it. When I got out of the Jeep, she just sat there. I sighed, slammed the door shut and headed to the back to unload. Mitch slipped out of the tent and headed over to help unload. He glared at Krisztina then shot me a look.

I shrugged. "She helped load."

He raised an eyebrow. "Yeah, well there's still work to do." He stormed around the Jeep and yanked the door open. His chest expanded as he towered over her. Silently, she slid out of the Jeep and came around back to help.

I brought out another of the pop-up tents and handed it to Mitch. "We'll just store everything in here until we can sort it out tomorrow if you're too tired." We had filled the reusable shopping bags as we ran through the store this time, an initiative that would shorten the task of emptying the Jeep.

He shook his head. "We slept today, you didn't." He shot a glance in Krisztina's direction then tossed me a package of wet-wipes. "Why don't you wash up and get some sleep, we won't be far behind you."

I looked down at my filthy clothes. "I think I need more than a few wipes. I'm gonna try out the springs." I opened the back door and rummaged through a pile of clothes for a t-shirt and pair of sweat pants. This would have to do.

I made my way down the dirt trail in the fading light then climbed onto the rocks at the water's edge. After shedding my clothes, I held on to the guide ropes as I eased my achy body into the hot water, grateful for the instant soothing effect. I settled into the basin, rinsed out my dirty clothes and laid them on the guide ropes to dry.

This particular pool could not have been more than ten feet in diameter, maybe two feet deep around the edge and barely five feet deep in the middle. Fortunately, this was a hot spring, and not one of the smelly mineral springs. I wondered how smelly they were. I let myself drift off for a few minutes enjoying the soothing effects.

The sound of Mitch and Krisztina arguing crept into my awareness. I let out a sigh. So much for my quest for solace. The bitter memory of being designated peacekeeper came back. I had learned to be useful at a young age, helping my parents keep things flowing as smoothly as possible while they did their work. It wasn't easy when I didn't even speak the language, yet I had been expected to anticipate people's needs and make sure those needs were met. I never got to be a kid and it looked like things weren't about to change.

Hauling my tired and aching body from the water, I dried off quickly, stepped into the sweats and pulled the clean t-shirt over my head. I slipped my bare feet into my shoes and made my way reluctantly back to the tent. They were arguing about her not helping with the baby again. I ignored them and headed for the new supply tent and rummaged through the items. "Where'd you put the pop-up bed for the baby?"

Mitch poked his head inside. "It's still in the jeep; I figured we were going to set it up." He pulled back to continue his *discussion* with Krisztina. "Don't suppose you know how to set one up." The sarcasm in his voice was thick.

I stepped out of the tent and stared at the two of them. "We probably shouldn't have any lights on. It might give us away, so stop the bickering and let's get a move on."

* * *

Somewhere in the dead of night, I heard someone whimper. It took me a moment to remember where I was, to remember what had happened. Without turning on a light, I listened for the sound that I assumed had been the baby. I could hear the gurgling of the hot spring in the distance along with the steady breathing of the people in the tent. Someone sniffled and coughed before letting out another sound of distress. Jamie.

I reached out to my left, to where he had been sleeping, but his bedding was empty. Damn. In the dark, I slid out of my sleeping bag and crawled out of our room. Feeling my way to the door, I took a flashlight by the entrance of the tent, which I had no intention of using if I didn't have to. I slipped on my shoes and stepped out of the open tent door. Moonlight bathed the surroundings in an eerie light and the absence of night sounds didn't help my growing sense of unease.

Following a rustling noise behind the tent, hoping yeah there really were no animals left, I stepped into the darkness of the woods. The whimpering grew louder. "Jamie?" I called in a hushed voice. "Stay where you are, I'm coming."

He was crying, and I could hear him shivering. I cautiously felt my way around a large rock, touching the cold damp moss that covered its surface. My foot hit something and I almost tripped over the small figure huddled on the ground. I dropped down beside him, bringing him closer for warmth. "What are you doing out here in the dark?"

He sniffled and moved in closer. His voice was unsteady as he tried to speak through muffled sobs. "I wa– want my mom, I want to go ho– home. I don't like it here. Mitch said we were playing a game, but I don't want to play anymore." His voice cracked.

"Shh, it's going to be OK." I really didn't want to lie to him, because there was no way I could be sure it would be all right. I lifted him into my arms and moved slowly back toward the tent. A formation of lights streaking across the sky caught my eye and my body stiffened enough to get Jamie's attention.

"What's wr–" he started.

"Shh!" Oh God, oh God…please don't let them find us!

Chapter Four

"Don't move," I whispered, dropping to my knees. I held him tighter as I pressed my back against the nearest tree. My heart pounded in my chest as we sat there and waited.

Slow, almost deliberate footsteps could be heard moving towards us. Jamie buried his face in my neck and shuddered. My arms tightened around his small frame as I listened for the footsteps. My blood ran cold and the hairs on the back of my neck prickled. I opened my mouth, trying to breathe without making any noise, but Jamie's wheezing was getting louder.

Another step brought the intruder closer.

My heart pounded in my ears, making it difficult to judge the distance. Jamie coughed, and I'm sure my heart stopped. I kneaded his shoulders, trying to calm him, but I was so terrified I doubted I did any good.

The footsteps pivoted, hesitated and moved directly toward us. "Jamie," Mitch's hushed voice called out.

Relief washed over me, bringing a wave of dizziness in its wake. "Here," I croaked out shakily. "We're down here." I really didn't think I could stand.

I felt Mitch's hand touch my head before he dropped down on one knee beside me. Jamie turned to his brother and Mitch scooped him into his arms, stood and offered me a hand to my feet. I followed him back to the tent on wobbly legs, my heart still racing.

Moonlight filtered through the trees, making the tent visible. We were going to need a shelter that wasn't bright orange or had reflector strips on it.

By the time Jamie had taken his inhaler and settled back into his sleeping bag, the sky had started to lighten. Being mid-June, the nights were blessedly short. J.J. began to fuss and Ally appeared in the common room to rummage through the box of baby formula. I reached for the bottle and unscrewed the top, allowing her to attach the nipple. She gave me a weary smile before disappearing back behind the curtain on her side of the tent. Mitch came out from our side of the tent and I shook my head towards the door, inviting him to follow me out.

Heading straight for the supply tent I dropped to my knees and pulled out the stove and coffee pot. Mitch frowned. "Is that for Jamie?"

I shook my head. "I need it." I smiled weakly.

"Me too." He helped set up the stove and opened a bottle of water to fill the coffee pot. "What do you suggest we do today?"

I let out a sigh. "I think we have enough gas to make another run to the Wal-Mart store, but to be honest, I'm a little freaked by what I saw last night." I looked at him. The flicker of fear in his eyes confirmed that he'd seen them too.

"I was sure they'd taken Jamie," he whispered, suppressing a shudder. The color drained from his face.

"I don't mind telling you that you scared us good too." I sat back on my heels as the coffee pot began to perk, and then shifted around to face him before letting out a sigh. "I wish you could come with me to the Wal-Mart, but I wouldn't feel safe leaving the kids with Krisztina.

He nodded in agreement. "What do you want me to do while you're gone?"

I turned to look past the hot spring towards the cliffs and pointed. "See that rock formation, the slab of granite jutting out like a roof?"

He looked out at the cliffs. "Yeah, what about it?"

"Could you check it out and see if we could use it as a shelter?" I thought about our requirements for a moment. The tent would be fine for now, but I remembered hearing stories about how cold it gets and how much snow falls here in Montana, and if that's true, a tent wouldn't do. "We could build walls across the front and use it as a permanent shelter."

"Build walls with what?" He looked at me like I was nuts.

I pressed my lips together, thinking about what I had seen people living in over the years. From heaps of garbage, straw huts to tin shelters, clay houses and more. In fact, we didn't have it nearly as bad as some of the others I'd helped over the years. "Logs, trees, clay," I said. "If there's enough room under that slab for us to move about, I'd say we were lucky."

Mitch half nodded, half shook his head and let out a puff of air before passing his hand through his hair. "It's not like we have much of a choice." He looked at me. "I hadn't even considered winter." He looked down at his dirty jeans and sweatshirt. "We don't even have winter clothes."

I reached for the blue and black enamel coffee pot and poured two cups. I shut off the single burner and glanced into our makeshift supply tent. "I have no idea what to take from the store." I handed Mitch a cup. "We need so much stuff and the jeep doesn't hold all that much, considering this might become a very long term arrangement."

He put a hand on my shoulder. "I trust you."

I gave a half-hearted smile. His comment only added to the pressure I already felt.

* * *

As I cleared the wooded area and steered the jeep down the steep road, the town Krisz and I were headed to came into view. I pulled over onto the side and grabbed the binoculars to get a better look. The orange powder, or mist, looked like a sheer curtain, hanging from the heavens. Strangely, it came down perfectly straight and unwavering across the distance. It moved slowly but surely forward, leaving the fallen buildings looking like perfectly leveled gravel and nothing more.

We should be able to get in and out of the store long before the mist arrived, but this would definitely be the last time we'd make the trip. I offered the binoculars to Krisztina but she shook her head and turned away. I shrugged, started the engine and headed towards town.

Once again Krisztina and I headed off in different directions when we got into the store, each with a stack of reusable shopping bags ready to be filled in our carts. We had all but cleaned out the canned food and non-perishable sections of the store on our last trip. I grabbed camping and outdoor essentials along with extra sleeping bags. Being June, all the summer gear was out, but there was little that would be of help keeping us warm over the winter.

When Krisztina met up with me at the Jeep I had already unloaded two trips worth of items into the back. Krisztina opened the back door on her side and filled it up from floor to ceiling with her things. I paused at the stack of baby diapers that covered the floor of the backseat. "Don't you think you overdid it with the diapers?" I asked as I rolled the clothing tight and shoved it into the rooftop storage bag.

"What's that?" Krisztina looked at the balls of yarn I was packing into the black canvas bag. "Are you seriously packing balls of yarn?"

"Yeah, why?" I shot her a look that challenged her to complain about it and she let it go. Turning my face to hide my smirk I focused on the task at hand. The storage bag Mitch had found was huge and if I remembered correctly, it gave us almost nineteen cubic feet of extra storage. We needed every inch.

Once we had stuffed the Jeep beyond capacity, we made our way back to the mountain. Krisztina had been staring at me most of the ride home. I let out a sigh and turned to her. "If you have something to say, then say it. We might be stuck together for a long, long time and we're all going to have to work together if we expect to survive." I turned my attention back to the road.

"Did you really pack knitting needles?" she asked cautiously.

"For sure," I said matter-of-factly. "Along with a how-to book. The weather is nice now, but we're all going to need something warmer once the snow gets here."

Her eyes widened, but she said nothing.

The tents were empty when we got back. I nodded for Krisztina to follow me as I headed for the hot spring and the cliff. Mitch had dragged fallen trees, stripped of their branches, and was laying them out under the slab of stone. His eyes lit when he caught sight of us. "This is awesome!" He jumped down and hurried over.

My eyes searched for the others. "Where are the kids?"

Mitch's grin spread across his face. He nodded back toward the cliff with his head. "Come see."

I could feel Krisztina hesitate before curiosity got the best of her. I had hoped the slab could be used for some sort of shelter but I had never expected something so perfect. We could easily walk into the face of the cliff. The slab was almost ten feet high at its aperture and sloped down easily into the cliff, stopping about four feet from the ground at the back. Mitch had laid out the fallen trees as division markers. The kids sat in back, playing with rocks and sand. J.J., with a bottle of milk hanging out the side of his mouth, slept soundly on a blanket. Mitch waved his arms, explaining his vision for the space. "This is a perfect spot. We can sleep near the back and have a living area up front." He walked around the trees, or skinny logs he'd laid out, heading to the back of the area. "We can make storage areas near the lowest part in back by building walls or some kind of shelves in front of it."

Krisztina scoffed. Both Mitch and I turned to face her. She made a face and pointed to Mitch. "I hope you've watched plenty of those *home-reno* shows, 'cause this place is going to need it."

I raised an eyebrow and shrugged. "From the way I see it, you can help and earn your space within, or you're welcome to the tents once we've transferred here."

She opened her mouth but said nothing. Turning on her heel she headed back towards the Jeep. "I'm going to unload."

I looked at Mitch. "Should we just unload it all here and save us the trouble of doing it twice?"

Mitch nodded. "Can I drive the Jeep over?"

I pressed my lips together, suppressing a grin. "Keys are in the ignition."

"Aleksei, come see what we did," Jamie called out.

I went over to Ally and Jamie, and sat down on the ground next to them. J.J. let out a satisfied sigh in his sleep. His mouth moved as though he was still sucking on the bottle that now lay at his side. I turned back to the two others. "What did you want to show me?"

"Look." Ally pointed to a layout made of rocks and twigs. "We can make our room here," she said as she pointed to a 'room' on the far left of their rectangular creation. "You and Mitch get the room next to us and...*she* can have the room over here." She shot a look down in the direction of the tents.

"Why can't Krisztina share a room with you?" I watched her expression change slowly.

Her grey-blue eyes met mine before she dropped her head to stare at the ground. "She's scary, and I don't think she likes us much." She let out an exaggerated sigh.

We all turned as the Jeep approached. It came to an abrupt halt and rocked on its wheels before Mitch turned off the engine. He jumped out and called to the kids for help. Eagerly, Jamie and Ally scrambled to the side of the vehicle, ready to give a hand.

I looked around then turned to Mitch. "Where's Krisztina?"

Mitch looked up and shrugged. "Don't know."

I felt the sting of anger rise inside. We had lots to do and didn't have time for nonsense. "Did you say anything to her?"

Mitch stiffened before turning to face me with an armful of stuff. His face darkened and he spoke slowly and deliberately. "Not a word."

I let out a sigh. Damn, the last thing I needed was to get on Mitch's bad side. I grabbed stuff from the Jeep and chased after him. "Sorry, I didn't mean to accuse you of anything." I dropped the stuff down near the stone wall and headed back after Mitch. As I caught up to him by the Jeep, he turned to face me. "I'm a little overwhelmed right now." I gave him a weary smile. "I'm sorry."

He nodded and grunted, then grabbed another load of stuff and headed back to the rock ledge.

Ally ran into my legs and wrapped her chubby arms around them. She looked up with a big smile. "What can I carry?"

I tousled her hair and dropped down beside her. "Who is going to watch the baby while you work?"

She straightened. "I do one trip, and then I watch the baby while Jamie does the next one."

"Well then let's get you loaded up." I handed her two bags of bulky blue yarn, just enough to fill her little arms without weighing her down. "Go slowly and carefully not to trip."

She nodded as she made her way back to Jamie.

Krisztina came up behind me quietly. She twisted her hands nervously as she pointed back towards the tents. "I heated stuff for lunch," she said, color rising in her cheeks. She turned and headed back to the tents without another word.

Mitch and Jamie walked over to where I was. "What'd she say?" Jamie asked.

"She said it's time to eat," I answered him. I didn't think I'd figure Krisztina out any time soon.

"But no!" Jamie protested. "I didn't get to bring anything yet, and it's my turn!"

Mitch handed Jamie an armful and grabbed more for himself. "We have to go tell Ally to come eat, so we'll all make one more trip."

I pulled out some of the tools I had collected from the store and carried them to our future home. Jamie's eyes lit when he saw

36

them. "Cool," he exclaimed. "Can I help too?"

Mitch laughed and nodded. "Everyone will have to help."

I nodded as I bent to scoop up the still sleeping J.J. "Lunch time," I said as I herded the younger ones back towards the tents. I watched as they ran ahead, giggling. "I hope their attitude rubs off on Krisz."

Mitch walked beside me in silence. He passed his hand through his hair and looked back over his shoulder. "You really think this can work?"

I paused a moment to look at him and sighed. "It's not like we have a choice."

"How are we going to do it?" The expression on his face showed how overwhelmed he really felt.

"I've seen people living in scrap piles, even in winter time." I shuddered as I remembered seeing people with rags wrapped around their feet as they trudged through the snow. I sincerely hoped we wouldn't have it as rough. "I think we're lucky to have this to start off with. Besides, during the civil war these kinds of shelters were common."

"That doesn't tell me how we're going to do it."

"We'll make the front like a log cabin and fill in the cracks with clay and moss."

Krisztina had settled the younger members of the group down, each with a bowl of soup. She moved off to the side when we arrived and chose to sit by herself. Mitch shot me a glance and I raised an eyebrow. "Join us," I said. "We have things to go over."

Krisztina made a face. "How does that concern me?"

Mitch let out a snort. "Are we gonna have to go through this each and every time?" He shook his head in disgust and spooned some of the soup into his mouth.

Krisztina looked at me. "What exactly do you expect of me?" She stood up in a huff.

"Drop the attitude and sit down," I said, surprised at my gruffness. I passed a hand over my eyes. I didn't even know if *I* could do this. "Do you think I came with a know-it-all manual or something?"

"You're obviously the leader of the group," she said as she sat back down.

I lowered my head, shaking it in disbelief. I shifted the sleeping baby in my arms and pointed to Jamie and Ally. "Take a good look at those two. They have been pulling their weight since the beginning, and without so much as a complaint."

"Yeah," Mitch interrupted. "Thank God, too, because you've done enough whining for the entire group."

Krisztina's cheeks turned bright red, though I wasn't sure if it was from anger or shame.

Chapter Five

The next three weeks flew by. The weather had been pretty good and we had managed to form the outer wall of our shelter. Using twine, wire and nails we tied the logs together and filled in the cracks with a mixture of mud, clay and moss. On the second to last row of the wall I left spaces to insert a few half-gallon plastic bottles filled with water and a bit of chlorine that would illuminate our shelter. Jamie and Ally were filling the transparent soda bottles for me. Mitch and Krisztina watched as I added a bit of chlorine to the water before closing it. Slipping the bottle through the allotted space at the top of the wall I added moss and mud to seal it in place.

"That's it?" asked Krisz.

I nodded. "It allows for full spectrum light to pass through and gives about as much light as a 50w bulb. Fortunately, being on the south side, we get the maximum sun exposure possible for our bottle-lights. It'll help us save candles and batteries for when they'll be absolutely necessary."

Jamie handed me the last bottle. "Are you sure it's going to work?"

I smiled and handed him the bottle back. "Climb up the ladder and set it in its place." I held the makeshift birch ladder as he made his way up. "Remember how dark it was inside before?" I asked Ally.

Ally nodded. "It was kind of scary." She stared as Jamie stuffed the mud and moss around the bottle.

I helped Jamie down from the ladder and dropped to one knee by Ally. "Do you think you'd be brave enough to go in and *tell* me if it works?"

She twisted her mouth and straightened her shoulders. "OK, but you stay right here, just in case." She spun around, sending her disheveled curls flying.

Mitch chuckled softly. "Is this something your father taught you?" he asked me.

I nodded. "It's been used in a few countries to light up homes. We don't have as much daylight here, especially in the winter, but it's not like electricity will ever be an option for us."

As soon as Ally stepped inside Mitch closed the door behind her. "So? How does it look?" he asked Ally.

"Whoa," Ally said from inside. "You've got to see this!" The door jerked open and scraped across the stone floor to let us in.

From inside, each of the seven bottles glowed brightly, lighting up the entire area. Kristina spun around, looking at the lit interior. "How are we going to light up our rooms?"

"We won't be making full walls to cut the rooms off from one another. Maybe just partial ones because it'll be better to share the heat and light," I said. Why couldn't they do some creative thinking? I was half expecting Krisztina to argue about the walls.

Krisz nodded slowly. "Makes sense."

Mitch raised an eyebrow but kept silent. Wow, maybe we were making progress. He turned back to me. "How's the planting coming along?"

I crossed my arms over my chest. "There's still a lot of work to do, but the first plot has been planted. Why?" He had been cutting trees and stripping them of leaves, bark and branches while I tried to create a suitable planting bed.

He shrugged. "Now that the exterior wall has been completed, I think we should all pitch in and work outside when the weather's nice, and work on the interior on rainy days."

Krisztina moaned. "There's got to be something else for me to do. Ugh, I hate gardening." She plopped down on one of the camping chairs inside their shelter. Lifting her foot to the edge of her seat she propped her elbow against her knee and chewed absently on her thumb nail.

I started to pace the area. "Look," I said to her. "We are going to need food. Most of the city has been destroyed and there are no animals around." I watched Krisztina's face turn with disgust. "Whatever we can grow and eat now will leave that much more for winter. Once we're out of canned and pre-packaged food, we're out."

Krisztina looked up at me. "That's why you took all those seeds from the store?"

I nodded.

J.J. woke up with a start, screaming. I went over to the portable bed and looked down at him. His cheeks were red and had a bit of a rash. Picking him up I could feel his little body was warmer than usual. He was chewing on his pudgy fist with fury and drooling. "Where's the diaper bag," I asked no one in particular. There were teething drops in it.

Krisztina brought it over, eyeing me meekly. "I could stay and watch the kids while you and Mitch work outside," she offered.

Jamie spun on his heel, his face contorted in an overly dramatic way. "Do we got to stay here?"

I passed my hand over my eyes. I still wasn't comfortable leaving Krisz with the kids, even though we wouldn't be far…and I knew she had only offered because she didn't want to have to do the hard work.

Ally slipped her hand into mine. "We can take turns. Jamie can do some and I'll stay, and then I'll help when he gets tired." I tousled her hair and gave her a quick hug.

"OK, Jamie," Mitch said. "Make sure you have your water bottle, gloves and a hat." He turned to Ally. "Call *me* if there's anything." He shot Krisz a look of warning.

After having spent the rest of the afternoon in the field, we had another sizeable plot ready for planting. On our hands and knees we pulled and unrolled the top layer while Jamie or Ally would shake the dirt from the roots. It was a long, slow process but it would be worth it in the end. The previous plot, where we had planted root vegetables, had sprouted. Jamie and Ally showed genuine enthusiasm when they had noticed the appearance of the first sprouts.

Mitch and I sat on a rock overlooking the area. To the right was the hot spring, a little farther back and dead center was our shelter and our garden on the left. We had found a mountain stream where we could get fresh water and I had been picking wild roots, shoots and leaves for food. Getting the group to eat the steamed cattails had been a challenge, but in the end they had liked it. As convenient as it was to open a can of soup or stew, we really couldn't afford to overlook all that nature could provide us with.

Mitch picked up his water bottle and downed it in one gulp.

Using the bottom of his dirty t-shirt he wiped his face, removing a layer of grime and sweat. "I think we should get everyone to wash up and soak a few minutes in the hot spring before supper."

"Do you want me to go get them?" I stood up and stretched.

Mitch stood, grabbed the folding chairs and headed for the shelter. "Go throw yourself into the water and I'll be up in a few."

I shrugged and headed off towards the water. Using a pail I scooped up some of the warm water as I stood on the smooth stone edge. I stepped behind a makeshift screen, stripped down and washed myself using a bar of soap and a pail of warm water from the spring. I rinsed off and headed for the soothing warmth the hot spring promised. I eased myself in, letting the warmth relieve my tired body.

About ten minutes later Jamie came running up and tossed me a bathing suit and towel. "Mitch said you forgot this."

I pulled on the swimming trunks and rose out of the water. "Aren't you going to wash?"

He nodded glumly. "Mitch said I have to, but I get to go last." His jeans and jersey were filthy. Matted and hanging in his light blue eyes, his white blonde hair looked as dirty as his clothes. A bath would definitely not be a luxury in his case.

The next few days were rainy and dismal. Mitch and I had completed the planting of our second plot in the rain and hurried back to the shelter to dry off. Even though we were at the beginning of July, without the warmth of the sun it felt cold and damp in our makeshift home. Inside, Krisztina and the kids had been binding long branches to make the half walls and a worktable.

Our shelter gave us a good eleven feet of freestanding area from front to back before we had to stoop as we moved toward the back. All of our collected items were placed randomly at the back of the shelter until we sorted it into a more practical manner. For now, almost everything remained in the reusable bags. We had taken every candle, tea light and bottle of lamp oil we could find. A propane lantern lit the area, giving off a bit of warmth on such a dreary day. We would have to get started on building a fireplace so we didn't freeze over the winter. I just wish I knew how to build one.

"Can we do something else now?" Jamie asked miserably.

"Well, I did bring a few things from the store for rainy days." I had everyone's attention now. "Why don't you look through the red and orange bags to choose something while I play barber for a while."

Ally scooted over towards me. "Can you cut my hair short? I don't want it to be tangled anymore."

I pressed my lips together. I had helped with simple boy cuts or shortened lengths on girls, but this would be my first curly haired customer. At times a knife or straight edge was used to shear off the unwanted hair. I dropped down on one knee. "Will you forgive me if I don't get it right the first time?"

She shifted onto one leg and propped a pudgy fist on her hip. With a flick of her other hand to indicate her hair she asked, "Do you really think it could be any worse?"

Everyone laughed.

I motioned to a chair and bowed. "Take a seat, my dear. I'll see what I can do."

Ally covered her nose and mouth as she giggled and climbed onto the camping chair. I began cutting her sandy colored curls, letting them fall to the floor. In the background I could hear Mitch and Jamie as they colored in a book. I glanced up and saw that J.J. was playing in his travel bed while Krisztina sat in the corner with her back to the group. "Why don't you read something, Krisztina? I brought several books and magazines."

She lifted a shoulder in a shrug but made no move to turn.

I let out a breath. I think we're going to have to instate group meetings. I gave Ally a final look, placing the short curls around her face. Bandage scissors were not the instrument of choice, but they had cut well. She looked cute. "You're all done. You can go color with Mitch if you like."

She paused, putting a finger to her mouth. "Could I see the books you have to read? I just started reading this year and I like it." Her eyes held mine as if waiting for permission.

I went to the back of the room where our supplies were. "Come see what I have." I laid out a few beginner readers and activity books. "Take the one you want."

She nodded with enthusiasm and dropped down to the floor to examine the books.

"Jamie, you ready for your haircut?" My eyes were still on Krisztina. Was she crying?

"Can I finish my picture first?" he asked. He didn't bother looking up from his coloring page.

"Please?" Mitch prompted.

"Please, Aleksei?" Jamie corrected.

I turned to look at him, a smile tugged at the corners of my mouth. "Sure." I turned back to Krisz. Should I go over or ignore her? Well, I'll try anything once. I moved discretely closer to her and lowered myself to her level. She was definitely crying. "You want to talk about it?"

She shook her head and turned away.

Mitch looked up at me, asking 'what's wrong' with his eyes.

I shook my head. Bringing my attention back to Krisztina I gently laid a hand on her shoulder.

She pulled away with exaggerated force. "Don't touch me," she seethed. Her tears flowed freely now. She brought her knees up to her chest, shutting me out.

"What's wrong?" I asked. Everyone was watching her now.

"What's wrong?" she asked, her tone escalating. "What's wrong?" She dropped her feet to the floor and stood, pointing to the torn knee of her jeans. "Look at my pants," her voice cracked. "They're ruined and I can never replace them. Are we going to end up naked?" she stood and began to pace in the dim light. "How long are we going to be stuck here? What do we do when our food runs out?"

Jamie looked up panicked. "Are we going to die?" His breathing was getting faster and he started coughing.

"Way to go, Krisztina!" Mitch took Jamie by the shoulders and began speaking softly to reassure him.

Ally started crying too. "My mommy died when J.J. was born…I don't want him to die too." Her lip trembled as she made her way to her brother and lifted him into her arms. Being pulled away from his toy, J.J. let out a howl. Perfect.

"Ally, put the baby back in his bed." I stepped over to her and held her close. "Let's all sit down a minute," I ordered. "Now."

Mitch wiped the tears from Jamie's eyes as he helped him regain control. I sat in a camping chair, Ally on my lap. Mitch did the same with Jamie and motioned for Krisz to pull her chair in closer. I set the propane light at our feet so we could all feel its warmth then I let out a sigh. Mitch nodded for me to start. "First of all, we are not going to die." Ally shifted in my arms, resting her head on my chest, below my chin.

"Do you promise?" Ally whispered.

"Yes, I do." I looked at Krisztina. "We are a team now, a family. Everyone has to help in some way to make things better for us."

"Even J.J.?" Jamie asked.

"No, stupid," Krisztina said brutally. "And you are *not* my family."

I raised my hand to hush Krisz and keep Mitch in his chair. "None of that talk, ever. As a team or family, we must always treat each other with respect." I felt nervous tension mounting inside of me. How did I find myself in a position of authority, and what would happen if I lost their respect? We really didn't need to be pitted against one another. I drew a calming breath and smiled as Ally slipped her small hand in mine.

"It's OK," she said only to me. "I'm here."

I hugged her close, feeling the sting of tears in my eyes. "Look," I said to the group. "The only way we're going to get through this is if we all stick together. There are lots of things that have to be done to make sure we get through the winter."

Jamie sat up straight on Mitch's lap. "But I thought it was summer."

I nodded. "It is, for now. We have a lot of work to do so that when winter gets here we'll have a warm place to sleep and food to eat."

Krisztina stared at the floor, shuffling a bit of dirt around. "Who says we're going to be here that long? What if they find us?"

Mitch looked at me before answering. "Then good for us, but I don't think I want to sit around hoping to be rescued, cold and hungry."

Ally tilted her head up as her grey-blue eyes met mine. "Do you think my daddy is OK?"

"I want to believe that all our daddies are OK. We never did see any—" I paused to choose my words carefully. "—badly hurt people lying around." I pressed my lips together tightly. I wasn't sure if I should mention what had been bothering me, but I figured we should cling to any bit of hope possible. "If everyone had disappeared, I can't help but think the GPS would not have worked."

Krisztina perked up. "Do you really think it could mean something?" She brushed her wavy brown hair from her face, her dark eyes hopeful.

Mitch nodded. "It makes sense. Maybe only our area was affected." Jamie let out a deep sigh and Mitch's hazel eyes dropped to stare at his now sleeping brother.

"Do you want me to bring you a cover?" Krisztina offered meekly.

Mitch didn't answer. He nodded so slightly that it would have been missed if she hadn't been watching.

I closed my eyes for a fraction of a second and offered a silent prayer of gratitude. Maybe we would make it through.

Krisztina boldly draped a polar fleece cover across Jamie's sleeping form. She avoided Mitch's eyes as she returned to her chair.

"Thanks," Mitch said in a low voice. He shifted Jamie in his arms and turned to me. "What exactly do we have to do to get ready for winter?" He looked around the room. "I get that we have to finish our shelter and that we're growing food, but how do you plan on keeping us warm?"

How do *I* plan on keeping us warm…I repeated to myself. I cleared my throat. "We need to make a fireplace." I pointed to the hole in the wall behind me. "It was not meant to be a second door, but a hole for the chimney."

"That means we need firewood," Mitch said.

I nodded. "Lots of firewood."

"How much food do we need?" Krisztina asked.

At least she was participating in the discussion. "Much more than what we have," I answered.

She opened her mouth than shut it in thought. "Shouldn't we try finding another store or something?" She wrung her hands nervously. "We've just been sitting here when we should have been collecting things from stores or even houses." She played with the tear in her jeans.

Mitch rose and went towards the back to lay Jamie on his sleeping bag. "I can head out with the jeep tomorrow. We might find something."

I nodded wearily. "We don't have much gasoline left, and I

wouldn't want you to get stranded." I let out a long, slow breath. "OK, you can try, but pay attention to where you go and if you haven't come across anything after half-an-hour, promise me you'll turn back."

Mitch nodded. "Sounds fair. Maybe we could check the GPS before going. Doesn't it show restaurants?"

"You're asking the wrong person. You forget that I have spent most of my life away from technology," I answered slowly. I felt a sudden pang of longing for all I had left behind. I forced a breath to try and calm myself.

* * *

In the morning, once breakfast was out of the way, Mitch and Krisztina prepared to head out with the jeep. Jamie fidgeted as his brother prepared to leave. "Why can't I go too?" he whined.

Ally joined Jamie and pulled on the hem of Mitch's shirt. "J.J. and I want to go too," she said in a subdued voice, her eyes hopeful.

Mitch looked at me and furrowed his brows. I shrugged. "We could all take a little drive. If we find anything worthwhile, we'll just load up like the first time."

Krisztina rolled her eyes. She was still wearing her torn jeans from the night before whereas Ally and Jamie both had on slightly oversized overalls that I had taken from the store.

Jumping up and down, they begged Mitch to let them come. I could see him forcing back a smile. "Fine, let's go for a drive."

Krisztina's mouth opened in protest but the look Mitch shot her worked. She closed her mouth, crossed her arms and stormed over to the jeep. I turned to Ally. "Is your brother ready to go?"

Sheepishly she reached beside his travel bed and produced a packed diaper bag. "I'll go get him," she said.

It was a beautiful day for a drive. Heading off in the opposite direction from our usual store excursions, we came across a small compound near the park's entrance. It looked like an old western town. The trademark missing walls from the attack were visible here too. Mitch pointed towards the buildings. "It's almost as though they knocked out one wall per building to get the people into the streets."

I nodded. "I was thinking the same thing." I leaned in closer and lowered my voice. "Still doesn't explain where everyone went."

Mitch nodded. "Stop over there." He pointed to one of the buildings.

I eased the jeep close to the building and stopped. Looking over my shoulder I saw that Jamie had nodded off. "Did you want to check it out?" I asked Mitch. "I'll stay here with the kids." Ally looked down at the sleeping baby in her arms and nodded. Reasonable beyond her years, I thought to myself as Krisz climbed out of the car.

Enjoying the silence I leaned my head back against the seat and closed my eyes. I could hear Ally shifting behind me and didn't jump when I felt her hand on my shoulder. I turned around to face her, surprised by the look on her face. "Are you OK?" I asked.

She gave a half smile. "I was just thinking 'bout my momma." Her eyes glistened with the threat of tears.

"Did you want to tell me about her?" I watched her consider my question.

"What was your momma like?" She inched forward on her seat, mindful of her sleeping charge.

"Well, my mother's a doctor. She used to be part of the Canadian Forces, and when her time was up she became part of the Doctors Without Borders program." I paused wondering if any of this made sense to her. "She went to many different countries over the years to help sick people in small villages."

"Did your daddy go too?"

"Yes, he helped build schools and taught the villagers to grow food." I remembered how serious each one took their job. "He grew up not far from here, actually."

Ally listened, considering his words. "Do you miss your momma?"

"I do."

"Momma never got to hold J.J.," she whispered, looking down at her brother. She sighed. "Daddy didn't want to…now he never will."

"Oh, Honey. We don't know that for sure." I reached out to touch her cheek. She squeezed her eyes shut, letting a single tear fall. I was in awe at how brave this little soul was.

The sound of Mitch and Krisztina coming back caught our attention. Their arms were laden with bags. "I'm going to give them a hand. Can you keep an eye on these two for a moment?"

She nodded.

"Be right back." I hurried from the car and opened the back of the jeep. Mitch stepped on the edge of the open door and opened the rooftop storage. "All this from a souvenir shop?" I asked.

Krisztina nodded enthusiastically. "You're so gonna love what we found."

I raised my eyebrows in disbelief. "Are there more bags?"

"Oh, yeah," she said with a smile. "Come on."

I followed her back inside and grabbed the bags by the door. Looking down I tried to make out what Mitch and Krisz had found.

"We got food, clothes, blankets and even some books so you don't poison us with those roots you've been collecting." She picked up an armful of bags and headed to the jeep.

A small display of jewelry caught my eye as I passed the door. I lifted the tiny angel pendant and removed the necklace from the wooden rack. I'd give this to Ally.

Mitch took some bags from my hand and stuffed them into the remaining spaces. "Do you think we should take anything else?"

"Wait!" I hurried back inside and grabbed a wooden table holding pamphlets. Letting the items slide to the floor I hauled the table to the jeep. We didn't have a decent table to eat on, and this would be perfect. Maybe we could scrounge around for some pieces of furniture later on. I noticed the display of candles had been emptied. Good. They were thinking the right way now.

Mitch hurried to help me and we slid two of the legs under the rooftop storage. So much for aerodynamics, but it would be a welcome addition to our home. "Cool," he said. He held up a finger, signaling me to wait and ran back inside. He came out with a few pieces of furniture and tossed them up top. "Now we can go," he said as he secured the bundle to the roof.

I shook my head and climbed in behind the wheel. Unless we found more fuel, this would be our last car ride. I started back toward our shelter, pausing as we came to the view over the valley below. My skin crawled at what I saw. Everything below had been reduced to rubble. Movement from the corner of my eye caught my attention. "Oh, Shit!"

I pulled the jeep off the road into some underbrush just as a formation of spacecraft flew below the ridge. My heart pounded out of control as a second formation flew over the road where we had been minutes before.

Chapter Six

We sat in the jeep for over an hour, afraid to move from our spot. The aliens were still here and I couldn't decide what was worse, driving in broad daylight, or driving at night with the lights on. Mitch was the first to break the silence. "I'm going to make my way closer to the ridge to see if they're still there." His voice sounded brave, but his hazel eyes gave away his uncertainty.

I nodded. I was sure everyone held their breath for what seemed like an eternity until Mitch came back. "Anything?" I asked.

He shook his head. "Not as far as I can see. We should head back." He looked around. "Try and keep us close to the trees for cover."

Although we had no more than a twenty-minute drive ahead of us it took much longer since every glimmer of light or imagined sound had us taking cover. Thankfully the road we travelled was through a heavily wooded area. By the time I pulled the jeep past the hot springs and up to our shelter, I was exhausted. J.J. had demanded to be fed on the way and Krisztina had helped out, afraid his cries would give us away.

"I'll carry the kids inside," Mitch said as I turned off the engine. "Then we can unload and hide the jeep"

I nodded, trying to relieve the tension in my arms and legs. I hadn't realized how tight I had been holding on to the steering wheel, but now I felt it. I watched Krisz carry the baby inside, leaving only a sleeping Jamie behind. I turned to unload the jeep while Mitch came back for his brother.

Stepping inside the shelter with an armful of supplies, I wondered how long we'd be sharing this space. I wondered if it was even worthwhile to try and stay here. The city had all but been destroyed and we still had no clue if anyone else had managed to survive. I let out a breath as I deposited the supplies on the ground. The shelter was slowly taking shape and becoming a home. The kids slept while Krisz actually started to prepare something for us to eat. Mitch squeezed by with a sleeping Jamie in his arms and I headed back for more supplies.

Outside, I leaned back on the side of the jeep, overwhelmed by our situation. Was it all for nothing? Then I thought about the people my parents had helped over the years. Our plight seemed nothing in comparison. For now, we were healthy, had an adequate shelter and enough food. We also had resources to go on for a time. I took in a sharp breath. This was no time for a pity-party. With a sigh I pushed off from the side of the jeep and grabbed another armful of stuff.

Mitch came out to help. "You OK?"

I nodded, giving a weak smile. "Yeah, I just needed a minute."

"Are you going to bring in the table?" Krisztina asked, poking her head out the door.

Mitch held up a hand. "We're going as fast as we can." He untied the furniture from the roof and pulled down the smaller pieces. "Here, bring this inside." He handed her one of the smaller tables.

Together we pulled down the large, wooden table and maneuvered it through the door. "Set it down here," Krisztina said, bobbing happily around the table. I'm never going to understand her.

After having unloaded, the three of us sat around the table eating while the younger ones slept. Mitch placed his hands on the table, fingers laced together, and looked at me. "How do you plan on building this fireplace?"

"Oh, wait," Krisztina said as she went to retrieve a book from the back of the shelter. "Here." She handed me an outdoor survival guidebook.

Flipping through the pages I saw that it covered everything from survival medicine to shelters, including fireplaces out of mud, sticks and stones. "This is going to be useful." I pointed to the diagram. "We're going to need lots of rocks." I looked at Krisztina. If you're not willing to garden, will you help carry rocks or mud?"

She made a face but nodded. "I welcome anything other than gardening."

Mitch snorted. "The hard part is done. Now we have to keep the weeds under control and care for the plants." He took the book and flipped slowly through the pages.

"I'll even give knitting a try if it means I don't have to work in the garden."

I shrugged. "As long as everyone contributes, and all the tasks are covered, it doesn't matter what you do."

Mitch slammed the book down. "I don't think she should be able to get out of chores that easily." He ran a hand through his hair. "There's work to be done, everyone should chip in."

I let out a breath. "If she was sitting around reading while everyone was working, I'd have a problem with it." I looked from Krisz to Mitch. "However, I think that if having her in the garden turns out to be more of a chore for us, then I'd rather she do something she enjoyed." I held up a hand to ward off his protest. "As long as she contributes."

Mitch glared at me. "I don't think she should get off so easily. It isn't fair."

Krisztina crossed her arms and sat back in a huff. The look I shot her held off her comment while I frantically searched for a suitable example. "Look Mitch, if she doesn't want to weed the garden, she can haul firewood. There are so many things to do right now that I think we can pick and choose to a certain extent." I held up a finger to hold him off a second while I made my point. "My mother worked as a doctor, while my father worked as a carpenter or a gardener. His job was in no way less important than my mother's. He worked just as hard as she did…and together they made a big difference in people's lives." I hoped it was enough for him to understand. "The guy who went around adding bottle lights to neighboring villages was no doctor, but his contribution was indispensable."

Mitch let out a breath in frustration. "I still think it's a cop-out."

"I think I deserve a chance," Krisztina said. "I'm in this too, you know."

Finally, I thought. She was beginning to accept her place in our group. "What do we do about the kids?" I looked back to our three sleeping babes. "Did you cook enough for them? I don't think they'll make it through the night on empty stomachs."

Krisz frowned. "There's enough, but they pigged out on moose nuts and river rocks. Their bellies are full."

I must have misunderstood. I shook my head. "They ate what?"

"Nut clusters and chocolate," Mitch clarified. "Any left?" He asked Krisztina. "I could go for some myself."

She nodded and went to find the packages from the gift shop. Laying the open packs on the table, she took some of each and handed it to me. "Try it."

"I realize we have enough on our agenda for the time being," I started saying between bites. This stuff was good. "But I think we should make an effort to continue both Jamie and Ally's education."

Both Mitch and Krisz stopped eating and turned to me. "Why?" she asked. "What's the point?"

I frowned. "What do you mean, 'what's the point'?" I couldn't hide the astonishment in my voice or my expression.

Krisz curled her lip. "Like we don't already have enough to do without adding to the load. Who cares if they don't learn math or reading?"

"I do, and I'm sure they do too." I said. I couldn't figure out if I was angry or annoyed with their attitude. "I don't suppose you know what un-schooling is, then." Since they were looking at me as though I had sprouted horns, I had my answer. I let out a sigh. "It means teaching through all we do, not in a conventional classroom setting."

Krisztina let her hand drop to the table. "Yeah, 'cause you never know when cooking cattails will become a required subject."

Mitch shook his head and leaned closer to the table. "No, I think I get it." He looked at me. "You mean like teaching math through everyday activities, like how many rocks to form the base of the fireplace, or how many rows high..." his voice trailed off. He wrinkled his brow.

"Exactly," I said, relieved. "Life becomes their classroom. We should, however, still take time for reading and stuff like that, but there's no reason they can't learn spelling by writing in sand or using sticks and stones to form letters."

Krisztina rolled her eyes. "Whatever."

I stood and went in back to fetch a ball of yarn, knitting needles and a book. I laid out the items in front of Krisztina. "I'm sure you've seen the basics in home-ec, so now it's time for you to put it to some use." I nodded for Mitch to join me by the wooden wall with the survival book in hand.

Using our shoes we marked off the base of the fireplace. "Should we knock out the section of wall or build the fireplace mostly outside?" Mitch asked, studying the various images in the book. He looked up at me, pointing to a picture. "This one is completely outside, and the inside of the fireplace is made of logs that were covered in mud. We wouldn't lose any indoor space."

I passed a hand over my mouth. How was I supposed to know which one to choose? "I know the book shows wood lining the chimney, but I find it a little scary."

Mitch shrugged. "They must know what they're talking about." He pointed to another page. "They also suggest we make a second wall, about a foot inside this one and that we fill the gap with dirt so it will act as insulation." He sat down, flipping through the pages.

I nodded, figuring the plans in my head. If we made the fireplace completely outside the shelter, with only the opening from our side, I would fear the possibility of a fire much less.

Mitch came over with the book, pointing to a paragraph. "They actually suggest making a fire at the back of a cave-shelter like ours, saying the smoke will rise and exit on its own."

"You're not serious." I took the book and examined the paragraph. I looked at him, trying to read his expression. "I would feel more comfortable making it here."

He raised his eyebrows, nodding. "Me too."

OK, at least I wouldn't have to fight him on it.

"I wouldn't want to have all that smoke in here because of Jamie's asthma," Mitch said. He looked at his watch. "I don't know about you two, but I'm wiped." He looked at Krisztina who was struggling with the knitting needles.

"Let me finish up this row," she said twisting the yarn around the needle. She slipped the last loop onto the opposite needle and put her creation down on the table with a satisfied grunt. "It's not as bad as I thought."

Mitch flashed me a grin with a raised eyebrow but thankfully kept all comments to himself.

* * *

By mid-morning, the wooden chimney started to take shape. Krisz had Jamie and Ally collecting branches along with her while Mitch and I notched the wood and fit the pieces together. I figured we'd have to stand on the table to finish the top of it. "We're going to have to make the hole in the wall bigger." I looked at the hole from inside. At least a foot on either side would have to be removed.

Mitch looked up from the three-inch thick branch he had been chipping at with an axe and wiped his brow. "Why don't you grab the saw and get on it? I'd like to start covering all this with mud as soon as we can."

I nodded, looking about for the saw. J.J. was standing in his pack'n play, chewing on the padded rail, watching Mitch work. "What's the matter?" Mitch asked me.

I made a face. "I can't find a saw and we had at least five of them." I ran inside to look around. The stuff we had collected lay strewn across the back of the shelter. I let out a sigh of frustration. Next project would be getting this place in order. I found the end of a saw sticking out from under bags of food. Shaking my head I pulled it out and headed over to the fireplace opening. "Hey, Mitch," I called out. "I need your opinion here."

No answer...

I stepped outside to find J.J. had been left alone. "Mitch?" Looking around I was unable to see him. "Krisz! Is Mitch with you?" I called out.

"No, just the three of us and we're almost done," she called back.

A stream of falling pebbles caught me in the shoulder. I spun around and looked up. Mitch was high above my head, climbing the face of the cliff. I pushed J.J.'s pack'n play under the ledge to protect him and took a few steps back to get a better look.

Mitch stepped onto a small outcropping and surveyed the area. I had no idea what he was looking at but I saw him stiffen as he leaned forward, trying to get a better view. The same way he had done when he first saw the orange powder falling from the sky.

"Come on, guys," Krisztina's voice came from behind me. "We're almost there."

I whirled around to see the group of them dragging branches behind them. Both Ally and Jamie struggled to haul their bundle out of the underbrush. I hurried to help them but Jamie waved me off. "It's OK, we've got it." He faltered and I reached out to steady him. He had a scratch across his cheek and both of them looked worn and tired.

"Stop." I lifted the end of their charge. This was way too heavy, even for two of them. "Go relax in the spring," I told them. "Just keep to the shallow end."

Ally hesitated. "Will we still get to eat if we stop now?"

Krisztina, who appeared behind the kids at that point, averted my gaze guiltily.

I raised an eyebrow at Krisztina. Turning back to Ally I reassured her. "You two go on, now. I'll fix dinner while you clean up and relax in the water."

Jamie's shoulders slumped with exaggerated exhaustion. "I thought we'd never get done."

"Go on and change," I ushered the two inside. "And don't forget to put your dirty clothes in the laundry bag." I turned on Krisz as soon as they shut the door behind them, not caring that it wouldn't do much to cut the sound of my voice. "What's wrong with you?" I clenched my fists as I stared at her in disbelief. "What did you think you were doing with them out there?"

Her mouth dropped. "You were the one who said everyone had to contribute." She threw the bundle of branches to the side.

"They are six and seven years old. Jamie is asthmatic." I spoke through clenched teeth, trying to keep from raising my voice. "A little bit of judgment and common sense on your part would be expected."

"You dump them on me and now you get mad about *how* I take care of them!" She clenched her fists in the air before stomping off. "I didn't do anything wrong!" she yelled over her shoulder as she stormed off towards the fields.

Mitch landed behind me, startling me. "What's with her now?" he asked.

I waved away his question. "Nothing." I turned to face him, looking for answers in his face. "What were you doing up there anyway?"

He closed his eyes and let out a heavy sigh. "You might want to climb up and see for yourself. I'm not sure how to describe what I saw." He motioned for me to follow. "You coming?"

I hesitated a moment. We'd be able to see Jamie and Ally from above, but I needed to be sure Krisz would keep an eye on the baby. "Give me a minute." I sprinted off to the fields and found

Krisz leaning over some of the plants, watching a ladybug. Some of the insects had started showing up again. "I need you to come back and keep an eye on the kids for a few minutes, Mitch wants to show me something."

She hesitated. "Oh, OK." She followed me back in silence as I sprinted ahead to meet Mitch.

I slapped him on the shoulder. "OK, show me." We climbed up to where Mitch had been perched earlier. Once we made it to the ledge he handed me the binoculars and pointed without saying a word. The hair on the back of my neck prickled as the scene came into focus. I handed the binoculars to Mitch and waited for him to come to his own conclusion. I sat down and on the ledge. What were they doing?

Mitch plopped down beside me. "It looks like they're turning the entire city into some kind of quarry."

I felt like throwing up. Crossing my arms over my knees I rested my head on them, then slowly turned toward Mitch. "So what do we do now?"

"I don't know," he said solemnly. "Do you think we're safe here?"

I shrugged. "There hasn't been any of that orange powder falling here. It's as if they've focused on the town." I had no clue. I sat up. "I wish I knew if there were other areas that have suffered a similar fate."

"What would it change?" Mitch leaned back and stared up at the sky.

"I say we keep on going, hoping we aren't alone and that somehow, someone will show up for us." I stood and brushed dirt off my pants. "Let's get back down to the others. I'll fix us something to eat."

He nodded and stood. "I keep hoping this is nothing but a bad dream, and that any minute now I'll wake up."

Jamie met us when we reached the ground, grinning from ear to ear. He held a bowl of raspberries in his hands. "Look what we picked!"

Taking a few I popped them into my mouth. "Wow, those are great. Thank you, Jamie."

"There are tons of them over there," he said, pointing past our garden.

"Tons, eh? Then we should make some fruit leather," Mitch said enthusiastically.

"What's that?" Ally asked, standing in the doorway.

Mitch smiled. "Come on, I'll show you the recipe in the book. You can help me make it."

"Me too," exclaimed Jamie.

I watched them head off, but I couldn't seem to shake the image of the destruction from my mind, or the feeling of helplessness it brought.

Chapter Seven

Pulling a wool sweater over my head, I settled on the 'front porch' in the dark. Hard to believe it was already fall. I felt as though I had missed out on summer completely with all the work we'd had to do, but at least now there was plenty of food stored and wood piled. The books Krisztina had found at the gift shop had proven to hold a wealth of information. We'd dried food, put the root vegetables in a bin of sand and made fruit leather from all the berries and apples we'd found. A semblance of a routine had been established…if you ignored the occasional clashing between Mitch and Krisztina which had a tendency to send one or the other stomping off and putting a hold on whatever they had been doing. On second thought, their clashing had become the only steady routine.

Letting out a slow breath, I picked up a piece of fruit leather to chew on. My breath hung in the air and a chill crept through me, reminding me that snow would be coming soon enough. A scraping sound above my head caught my attention. Mitch. Once again, he sat perched above my head on the rocky ledge, while everyone else had long since fallen asleep.

All was quiet…except for the sound of the hot spring and Mitch as he shifted his weight. He had become obsessed with what the aliens were doing, and try as I might, I couldn't get him to focus on anything else.

"You plan on staying up there all night?" I asked him. Both Krisztina and I had climbed up to get a look, and we had no desire to watch the destruction of the city. Inch by inch it was being turned into a deep and depressing quarry. How far would the aliens go? How many cities had been affected? What would happen to us? I sighed.

"I'm coming down now. I'm so cold I think I'm going to sleep by the fire tonight." He coughed as he made his way down the makeshift rope ladder.

"I'll go heat up some water for cocoa. It'll help warm you up." I stood and pushed open the door to our home. The smell of wood smoke and pine greeted me in the dimly lit room. The sound of deep breathing and the occasional crackle of the fire served as background music as I prepared the kettle. It was cozy in here.

Looking in on the sleeping group I found Jamie and Ally snuggled together on my side of the room, leaving Krisztina alone on her side of the shelter. I sighed, wondering what had brought that about again. J.J. was sprawled on his back in his portable bed, placed out in the open so he could benefit from the heat. I smiled as I watched him sucking on his lips in his sleep. When he was out, nothing could wake him, which was definitely a good thing.

Turning off the stove, I left the kettle full of hot water on the single burner. Mitch still hadn't come in. I frowned as I opened the door to see what was keeping him. He wasn't there. I stepped away from the door and looked up; hoping the sliver of moonlight would be enough to shed some light on the ledge above. He didn't seem to be there either. "Mitch," I called out in a hushed voice. Maybe he had gone to use the outhouse. We had made a compost potty, which smelled infinitely better than the more traditional type of latrine.

Rustling in the bushes caught my attention. I turned around to scan the dark wooded area but couldn't see a thing. The hair on the back of my neck prickled. "Mitch?" I whispered. Nothing. I hurried back to get a flashlight and jumped when I felt a hand on my shoulder. I spun around and came face to face with Mitch. Even in the poor light I could tell something was off. He held an arm across his abdomen and his forehead was beaded in sweat. He stumbled.

"I hurt myself," he said through clenched teeth.

I slid under his free shoulder and helped him into the shelter. Easing him into a chair I dropped down on one knee in front of him. "Let me see."

He removed the arm that had been across his ribs and I helped him out of his open jacket. Even in the poor light I could see the blood that had soaked through his shirt and covered his hand. Damn. "Climb up onto the table." I grabbed a blanket and folded it roughly, slipping it under his head. "What'd you do?" I undid the buttons from his shirt and eased it open. I needed more light. Mitch grabbed my hand as I reached for the propane light.

"Not that," he said. "It's too bright and you'll wake the others."

I passed a hand through my hair but nodded in agreement. Instead, I threw more wood onto the fire and let the flames light the room as I gently peeled his blood soaked shirt from his chest. My stomach lurched as I saw the extent of the damage. "What happened?" I felt my eyes widen, betraying my shock. My stomach turned as the smell of blood assaulted my nose.

"I fell on something in the woods, but I don't know what." He winced, biting back a yelp.

"Sorry." I grimaced, feeling for him. I really wasn't cut out for this stuff. Mom, help me if you can…

"How bad is it?" he asked through clenched teeth.

"You've got debris in the wound that has to be removed." I glanced at him, to see if I was hurting him as I gently pulled the tattered shirt fragments from his abdomen. "Hold on." I went to get the first aid kit and put on a pair of gloves. I used tweezers to remove pieces of wood or dirt from the wound below his rib cage. I wondered if there were any internal injuries.

Mitch began to shiver uncontrollably. He was probably going into shock, crap. "Hang in there." I put a hand on his shoulder. "I'm going to get you a blanket." I hurried back for a thick polar fleece blanket and draped it over him. His eyes rolled back and his head fell off to the side. My blood went cold. Reaching for his neck I felt for a pulse. Weak and thready, but he was still alive. I grabbed another cover and elevated his feet, then went to wake up Krisz.

I knelt down by Krisztina's sleeping form, gently nudging her shoulder. "Krisz, I need your help."

"I'm sleeping," she grumbled before turning over.

I shook her again. "Get up, it's an emergency." I insisted.

She sat up, whipped the covers aside and shook her head, mumbling. I grabbed her hand and pulled her to her feet. As soon as she stood, wearing only shorts and a t-shirt, her eyes were drawn to Mitch's still form on the table. "What happened?" She hurried over to touch his arm. Her eyes filled with tears. "Is he…?"

I shook my head. "No, he just passed out. "We have to clean and bandage his wound before infection sets in."

She nodded, keeping her eye on Mitch's face. "What do you want me to do?"

I nodded toward the stove. "Pour the water into a bowl and add a few drops of tea tree oil. Bring me one of the clean cloths and a few towels." I returned my attention to the wound. He would have a good bruise and a bad scar, but at least all the larger foreign pieces had been picked out and we might avoid an infection. "And bring the honey after you're done."

Krisz held the bowl for me while I eased a thick towel under Mitch's midsection. Dipping the cloth into the warm liquid I squeezed it over the open wound. I half expected Mitch to jump, but he lay deathly still. Krisztina shot me a worried look. "He didn't lose that much blood, so he probably just passed out from the shock of it," I reassured her.

"That really looks bad," Krisztina whispered. A lock of her unkempt hair fell over her eyes and she brushed it away with the back of her hand, trying not to spill the contents of the bowl.

"Set it down here," I pointed to the chair behind me. "Pull off his pants and shoes."

She recoiled at first but then moved tentatively to his feet without comment.

Once the wound had been cleaned I probed a little deeper to make sure nothing had been left behind. "Hand me the bottle with the blue star painted on it. It should stop the bleeding."

She stood very close, watching as I unscrewed the cap. "Could I do it?"

I handed it back to her. "Sure, just add a few drops to the wound and wait to see if the bleeding stops. If not, add one or two more." I lifted the cover to expose his bare leg and proceeded to check for any missed injuries. His knee was bruised, but other than that the leg was fine. Replacing the cover I moved to the other leg and exposed it. Meticulously moving across the entire surface, I concluded that this one was in better shape than his right leg. Moving up his torso I checked for more bruising and possible broken ribs. His abdomen remained soft, showing no signs of internal bleeding. "Hand me the scissors," I said without looking up. "Actually, you cut open his t-shirt and I'll hold him while you pull it out from under him. Check his back too, just in case." I waited for her to finish cutting then I pulled Mitch forward into a semi-sitting position.

"All clear," she said.

I eased Mitch back down and checked his head for any bumps or blood, probably something I should have done before moving him. Too late now, at least there didn't seem to be anything wrong with his head. "Did you get the honey?"

"I thought you were kidding." She made a face before going to the food shelf. "What do you need honey for?"

Without answering I squeezed some of the golden liquid into his wound, careful to cover the whole thing.

Krisztina's jaw dropped. Regaining her composure she grabbed my wrist. "What are you, mental?"

I removed her hand from mine. "Look it up if you don't believe me. We have to do everything we can to prevent infection." I put the honey down on a chair. Now grab his legs, we're going to move him to your room before the others wake up."

Letting out an exaggerated sigh Krisz stood at the end of the table and grabbed Mitch by the knees. I lifted him from under his arms. Boy was he heavy. "Hurry, I didn't think he was this heavy," I said through gritted teeth.

Mitch moaned and tried to move. Krisztina hushed him. "Just relax," she grunted. Her eyes widened, showing the strain.

"Almost there." I leaned over to lay Mitch down and checked his wound, making sure the bleeding hadn't started again after our not-so-gentle transfer. I sat back on my heels and watched Mitch breathe for a while. "Cover him up but leave the wound exposed, I'll put a dressing on it in a minute." I said to Krisz before I headed back to clean up the mess, not wanting to scare the kids who would probably be rising shortly.

Removing all traces of blood and first aid took no more than fifteen minutes and before I knew it everything was in order. Krisztina had remained with Mitch, so I went to check in on them. I did a double-take when I saw Krisz sitting cross-legged at Mitch's side, stroking his hair. She let her hand drop when she noticed my presence. I moved in and quickly dressed Mitch's wound. "I'm going out for a minute to get some air. You should get some sleep." I gave her a reassuring smile. "He'll be fine, he's sleeping now." My eyes looked over her face. "Thanks for the help." I turned and headed out of the shelter.

Cold air rushed around me as I stepped through the door, and I instinctively pulled the blanket tighter around my shoulders before settling into a chair. The sky had completely clouded over, and I sat in total darkness breathing in the crisp air. With my head leaning back on the chair I felt tiny droplets wet my cheeks. The wind picked up and sliced right through my layers, chilling me to the bone. OK, time to head back inside. I stood and stretched, taking one last deep breath before quickly closing the door behind me.

Heading to the fireplace I added a few more logs to the bright embers, sending a cascade of sizzling sparks shooting up the chimney, and a puff of smoke into our shelter. It was a good thing we had a stone floor. My eyes burned, a reminder of just how tired I was.

Moving quietly I looked in on Mitch. Krisztina slept at his side, drawing a wide grin from my part. I wondered how Mitch would feel about that. I dropped down beside him and did a quick evaluation. No sign of fever, pulse slow and steady while his breathing was that of someone in a state of deep sleep. I lifted the blankets that had slipped over the wound to see if there was any sign of blood. Good, all seemed well. Now I could go to sleep too.

By some miracle, the kids slept well into the morning, giving me a chance to catch up on my sleep. From far away I realized that Jamie and Ally were shaking me awake with urgency. "What's the matter?" I asked, scrubbing sleep from my eyes.

"We have to go and we don't have any snow boots to wear," Jamie said, doing the pee-pee dance.

Sitting up I shivered in the cold. Obviously Krisztina hadn't been up to add wood to the fireplace. I shook my head and tried to focus. "If you have to go, then go. You know the way."

Ally was tugging on my shirt. "Come see!"

I stood and pulled on my sweat pants along with a pair of wool socks. Jamie's dance became more frantic as I followed Ally to the door. Pulling open the door I was blinded by the sun's reflection on the blanket of snow that now covered the ground. I pursed my lips. "OK, now I see what you mean." When they said snow came early to the mountains, they weren't kidding.

Jamie was hopping around frantically. "Hurry, I gotta go bad!"

Hmmm. I'd deal with grammar later. I pulled out a pair of

rubber boots for each of them and draped a blanket across Jamie's shoulders. "I'll go with him first and I'll be back for you in a minute," I said to Ally.

"OK," she said cheerfully, taking a seat beside the door.

I picked up Jamie and carried him to the outhouse. While I waited for him to finish up I let my gaze pan over the landscape. It was breathtaking with snow-laden trees and bright blue sky. The air was so crisp, I wondered what it would feel like once winter did get here. I shivered. Now we could only hope we were ready, because there was no going back.

Chapter Eight

Winter had taken root with a vengeance. It was a good thing we had piled our wood as close to our shelter as possible, since just opening the door to bring in firewood left us feeling the bite of the icy air. Unfortunately, having spent the last few years in a tropical environment, I found it very hard to adapt to such a drastic change in climate.

"Looks like the snow is finally going to let up," I said, pushing the door closed behind me with yet another armful of wood.

Mitch took the load from me as I started to un-wrap the many layers of clothing needed to keep warm. It would have been so much easier on us had we found some stash of winter clothes at Wal-Mart. "The natives are getting restless," Mitch muttered under his breath as he stoked the fire. "We could barely get them to bed." He kept his voice low, careful not to disturb the others.

I hung my clothing on the makeshift coat rack by the fireplace and nodded passing a hand through my hair as I thought about a solution before we all got cabin fever. It wasn't going to be pretty in a few weeks.

Dropping to my knees by the fire I let the heat soak through the few layers of clothing I still had on. Damn it was cold. On a whim I reached for Mitch's arm and checked the date on his watch. Dec. 19th. I leaned in closer to Mitch, keeping my voice low. "How would you feel about getting ready for Christmas?" I gave him a moment to answer.

He tilted his head, letting the blonde strands fall over his eyes. "How could we pull it off?" He rocked off his knees and sat down on the braided rug beside me.

I shrugged. "Finding a tree is simple enough." I looked back toward the sleeping area, distracted by the restless tossing and turning of either Ally or Jamie.

Krisztina tiptoed from the back of the room, still holding J.J. in her arms. "He's finally asleep," she whispered, "but I'll wait before I put him down, just to be sure."

I turned back to Mitch, not wanting her to see me fight the urge to smile. I think the little man had weaseled his way into Krisztina's heart. "We can make decorations together, and we can find stuff from our reserves to fill a stocking for each of them," I said, returning to topic. "It'll be good for us to share in the preparations."

The corner of Mitch's mouth twisted. "What's the point?" He shook his head. "It's not like we could give them anything cool." His head dropped and his shoulders slumped as he let out a breath.

"I think you're missing the point," Krisztina ventured.

Mitch's head snapped up, mirroring my own surprise.

Krisz pulled up a makeshift cushion and she joined us by the fire. "Haven't you ever heard about the true meaning of Christmas?"

Mitch snorted. "Peace on Earth, good will towards men," he quoted, before rolling his eyes.

She closed her eyes a moment, shaking her head. Taking a deep breath she explained, "Every Christmas my father would slip away from the festivities and spend a quiet moment outside." Eyes still closed, her lips curled into a slight smile. "When I finally caught on to where he would disappear to, he shared the moment with me." Krisztina paused to inhale deeply. "It was truly wondrous."

"What are you talking about?" Mitch cut her off.

I held up my hand to silence him. "Let her finish." I turned to Krisztina. "Just get to the point, please."

Her head dropped and she shook it slowly. "There's just something special that you can feel on Christmas Eve." Her hand came to her chest. "You can feel it in here." She looked from Mitch to me.

I had seen more than my share of suffering, and I had been looking forward to celebrating Christmas with my father's family since I'd never had the picture-postcard, white Christmas, complete with a tree and turkey. "I hope you're right."

"What exactly do you have in mind?" Mitch asked.

Krisz smiled, and there was a glint of mischief in her eye. "Let's just prepare for the holidays as best we can, then maybe the magic will find you."

Mitch frowned. "We'll see." He stood and stretched. "Let's sleep on it and figure it out in the morning." He turned without another word and headed for bed.

I nodded, lost in my own thoughts as Krisz went to lay J.J. in his bed. Well, it wouldn't be the Christmas I had hoped for, but it might be nice to actually focus on the holiday and make something special for the kids. I pursed my lips. For myself, as well. Who was I kidding? I was getting excited just thinking about it.

Early the next morning, unable to sleep a minute longer, I set the dishes on the table while I waited for the others to rise. A pot of porridge hung near the fire and I placed bowls of dried fruit and nuts on the table. On a whim I laid out some pine branches and pine cones I had picked on my trek to the outhouse. Rummaging through our stash of candles, I found a huge red one that I placed in the middle of the table. This was going to be fun.

The sound of footsteps shuffling towards me drew me from my thoughts. I turned to see Ally staring wide-eyed at my set-up. Grinning, I dropped down to her level. "What do you think?"

She caught her bottom lip between her teeth and looked around before leaning in closer to me. "Does that mean Santa will find us?"

Her words tugged at my heart. "I don't know. Things are a little strange right now, but I think we can still celebrate together."

Her head tilted as she considered my words. "OK. I like Christmas." She looked around the room. "Can we get a tree?"

"You bet." I pulled out layers of clothing to protect her from the cold as per our morning routine. "We can make some decorations together."

"In school last year, we made spiced cookie ornaments to hang in the tree," she said as she bundled up. "They smell really good and you can eat them." She wrapped the extra long scarf around her neck and I fastened it for her. She looked like a heap of blankets with bright, grey-blue eyes peeking out.

As we made our way to the outhouse, I could see Ally looking around for a suitable Christmas tree. Sunlight glistened across the snow-covered pine branches. The view left me breathless; it truly was magical. The mountains stood majestically behind the tree line, and the deep blue sky seemed endless without the slightest hint of a cloud.

Movement in the trees startled me and my breath caught as I remained perfectly still, trying to see whatever had moved before it saw me. Besides, I couldn't leave Ally whom I could hear moving about inside the outhouse.

Squinting against the bright sunlight I caught sight of more movement. As if on cue, a black capped chickadee appeared from the dense pine trees to perch on a branch above my head. Relief washed through me. Since this whole adventure had started we had seen the progressive return of insects, fish in the river and now birds. I could only hope it was a good sign.

I turned back toward my charge. "How are you doing in there?" I leaned a little closer to listen for a response.

"Almost done," came her muffled voice.

Jamie appeared at my side, dancing on the spot. "She has to hurry," he pleaded.

"Come on out, Ally. Jamie won't last much longer." I ruffled his hair as the door pushed open. Ally was tangled in her layers of clothing. With a chuckle I lifted her into my arms. "I'll carry you back, it'll go faster."

"When can we get our tree?"

"After breakfast and chores," I blurted out automatically. Funny how some aspects of our lives had become routine...even in assuming parental roles with the younger ones. Before we had made it through the door, Jamie was on our heels.

"Are we really going to get a Christmas tree?" His forehead was twisted in a skeptical frown.

Ally pushed herself from my arms and turned to face him as I shut the door behind us. "Of course, silly. It's almost Christmas." I loosened my grip as she slid to the floor and immediately began to free herself from the many layers. "I'm gonna help make decorations for the tree," she said with a note of determination.

I raised my hand to head off Jamie's rant as his face twisted into frustration. "Everyone is going to help." I looked back at Ally. "Right?"

She nodded; then lifted her chin as she shot Jamie a glance. "But it's my recipe."

The corners of my mouth curled. "Yes, your recipe." I widened my eyes as I held Jamie's stare. "And then Jamie will be able to pick something from the books we have."

Ally pursed her lips. "I guess that's fair." She looked around the room. "Do you think the others have slept enough?

"We're up," came Mitch's sleepy voice. He stood and stretched before he made his way to the table. His hair stood mercilessly on end. He looked over at Jamie. "Do I have time to eat before I'm expected to cut down this tree?"

Jamie's eyes narrowed. "How much time do you need?"

I ruffled Jamie's hair. "Help me dish up so we can eat, then we will decide on today's schedule."

* * *

On Christmas Eve we sat in a semi-circle before the fire. We had shared a hearty soup, followed by a meal of roasted root vegetables along with some honey-glazed ham and roast duck that came in large tins from the gift shop. Our 'home' smelled of wood smoke, spices, pine and good food. Everyone seemed happy and serene as we watched the fire dance. The lit candles, placed strategically out of J.J.'s reach, added to the festive ambiance of the room.

Ally, who had snuggled in close, tilted her head up to look at me. I smiled down at her, planting a kiss on the top of her head. "What is it?" I asked.

She shrugged; then looked to the ground. "I wanted to sing Christmas songs, but I don't remember the words," she said in a muffled voice.

I nodded slowly. "Well, if I sing you something, would that help?" I lifted my eyes to target Mitch and Krisztina. "Then we can all sing together." I shifted and cleared my throat. "This is the Spanish version of *It Came Upon a Midnight Clear* that I sang in Guatemala last year.

A medianoche se oyó,
Aquel dulce refrán
De ángeles que en unión
Las gratas nuevas dan:
"La paz y buena voluntad
Del gran Rey celestial".
El mundo en quietud oyó
El son angelical."

I ended the song after the first verse and looked down at Ally. "What do you think?"

She nodded in approval. "You sing better than I thought," she said matter-of-factly, setting the room in an uproar of laughter. Even J.J. was clapping happily.

"Can we sing *Jingle Bells*?" Jamie asked.

"All together," Krisz added.

After a few shaky notes we were all singing in harmony, well together, in any case. My stomach fluttered with happiness and a sense of well-being came over me. Maybe Krisz was right, maybe there was something special about this night.

Krisz stood to pour juice for everyone. As we took a break from singing and focused on the mixture of powdered fruit juices, Krisztina shocked us all as she began to sing *O Holy Night*. Her voice filled the room, carrying us to another time, another place. She had the most amazing voice I had ever heard and when the song came to an end, no one said a word.

Mitch gave her hand a quick squeeze as she settled back down beside him. She wiped the corner of her eyes with the back of her hand and smiled weakly.

"Can you sing *Up on the Housetop*?" Jamie asked, shyly.

A small laugh escaped from her mouth as she straightened. "Sure, but you'll have to help me a bit," Krisz added.

A few hours later, each holding a sleeping child as the fire warmed us, we talked and shared a little of ourselves. "What did you like best about Christmas?" Mitch asked us both.

Krisztina's eyes misted as she shifted J.J. in her lap, but she didn't answer.

I thought about what I was feeling now and compared it to Christmas's past. "This is turning out to be quite a special holiday for me." I pressed my lips together in thought. "The one I've enjoyed the most, so far." I caught a flicker of emotion cross Mitch's face. "Don't get me wrong. I miss my parents, and not knowing what will happen to us frightens me. But if we're focusing on what I like about Christmas, then I like this." I waved an arm to encompass our group. "The teamwork, sharing, and caring."

Krisztina reacted this time. "You were living with missionary parents or something, right? So wasn't it all about teamwork, sharing and caring?" She glanced over at Mitch with a shrug.

I shook my head. "It wasn't the same. My parents focused all their attention on the people they were helping. We were included in the village or community activities, but it wasn't the same. I'd never had the chance to decorate a Christmas tree before, or prepare the meal or wonder what I could do or give as a gift." I cradled Ally with one arm as my free hand instinctively ran through her hair. "I have never felt any sort of anticipation for the holidays." A lump formed in my throat. "Watching Jamie and Ally take everything to heart as we prepared for Christmas was mesmerizing. It was magic. Even without the fancy lights and decorations, this place has been transformed into something wonderful." I let my eyes pan the room, following the flickering candlelight as it danced across our homemade decorations. Strings of popcorn, pine cones, small knitted mittens and hats adorned the tree. Paper snowflakes hung at varying heights from our clothes line at the ceiling, as per Ally's demand. I smiled. It wasn't as though we didn't have enough snow outside.

Mitch's face softened as he stared down at Jamie, brushing a lock of hair from his brother's eyes. "We're part of a huge family." He smiled weakly. "We all gather at Gram's house for the holidays, all forty-seven of us." He raised his head, a faraway look in his eyes. "Everyone is put to work decorating, cooking and setting up the extra rooms for those who come in from out-of-state. The older kids take charge of the younger ones, and we play games, sports, and some of the kids put on a pageant..." his voice trailed off.

We sat in silence for a moment before Krisztina spoke up. "This year it was going to be just me and Dad." She swallowed back tears. "We lost Mom last spring, and now I don't even know where he is," her voice was barely a whisper. "I wasn't looking forward to the holidays." She planted a soft kiss on the top of J.J.'s head. "If it wasn't for the circumstances, I'd really be enjoying this holiday experience." She wiped the back of her sleeve across her eyes.

I stretched, trying to get some feeling back in my legs. "What do you say we put these guys to bed, set out their gifts, and hit the sack?" Fatigue had started to set in and I was looking forward to curling up under my covers. I shifted my weight and dropped a knee to the floor for stability before rising to my feet. Ally stirred, snuggling in closer. My heart swelled, taking me by surprise. I'm not sure how or when, but I had somehow fallen in love with the mismatched family we had formed.

Mitch and Krisztina stood as well. "Good idea," Krisztina said, "I'm ready for bed myself."

"Same here," Mitch added. "Let's get our stuff done and call it a night."

* * *

The sound of whispering crept into my dreams, taking me away from a faraway land. Ally and Jamie were talking in hushed voices. I passed a hand across my face, trying to wake up enough to open my eyes. I could hear Mitch stir beside me before he grunted and sat up. Letting out a sigh, he forced a smile and nodded toward our early risers. "Come on, who knows how long they've been waiting."

Stifling a laugh I got up and stretched. "Let's go open presents."

Krisztina sat at the table in silence, watching the kids fidget beside the tree. With a twinkle in her eye, she nodded towards Jamie and Ally as she absently added pieces of food to J.J.'s bowl. "It's about time you two got up. They weren't going to hold out much longer."

Mitch looked around the room. "Why didn't you wake us?"

She shook her head. "They said they wanted to sit and watch the tree for as long as possible." She caught J.J.'s bowl as he swatted it off the table. "I made them a snack to hold them over, but if you let them open their gifts I'll set out breakfast."

While Jamie and Ally colored in their new books after breakfast, I decided to step out for some fresh air. I slipped out the door quickly, careful not to let too much cold air in. My gaze was drawn to the clear morning sky and I paused to fill my lungs with crisp mountain air, enjoying the moment. I turned to head down the path but my foot caught on something, sending me flying. Arms flailing, I tried in vain to break my fall but I hit the ground hard, just short of having the wind knocked out of me. Moaning, I rolled over onto my back and stared up at the sky. That hurt. My hand and knee throbbed. Wiping the snow from my face I sat up and pivoted to see what I had tripped over.

"What the…" I stood shakily and made my way back to the iridescent package that had lain across my path. Dropping down on one knee I passed a hand over the smooth, oblong surface. Pulling my hand back quickly, surprised by its warmth, I took a calming breath before reaching out again. It was warm, very warm, yet the snow it rested on showed no sign of having melted. I looked around for tracks in the snow or a sign that someone had left it here but there was nothing. It was almost as though it had been dropped here a second before I tripped over it. Gathering my courage, I laid both hands on it, looking to see if it could be opened.

"What are you doing?" Mitch's voice came from over my shoulder.

I jumped and clasped my chest. My heart pounded in my ears. "I tripped over this *thing*." I gestured over the object. "I was just trying to figure out what it was."

Mitch eased himself next to the object and tentatively reached out to touch it. He flinched, pulling his hand back as I had done.

"I don't think it's from around here." I turned to watch Mitch's reaction to my comment.

"Do you think it's a bomb or something?" he asked.

I hadn't even thought of that. I swallowed hard. "I was thinking it might have fallen off one of their ships."

A whooshing sound from the object startled us, sending us backward to the ground. Scrambling to our feet we stood, then cautiously stepped closer. The iridescent shell grew brighter and vanished, leaving a bundle of fabric at our feet. We stared at each other before crouching down to look through the pile.

"Winter clothes?" Mitch held out a one-piece ski-doo suit, about Jamie's size.

Reaching into the pile I lifted another smaller one out. "For Ally?" There was one for each of us, along with boots, hats and mitts. My mind raced.

"This is great!" Mitch exclaimed. He started to gather up the clothing, but I grabbed his arm.

"It means they know we're here," I said in a low voice, my throat having suddenly gone dry.

Mitch closed his eyes and drew in a forced breath. "What are you saying?"

I shook my head. I couldn't figure out if we were being helped, or if we had become someone's lab experiment. After all we had gone through, all the struggles, the worry and stress. Bile rose in my throat.

Gathering up the bundle, Mitch rose to his feet. "Come on. Let's bring this inside. No sense freezing out here."

I shot him a weary glance, and with a feeling of defeat, followed him inside.

The kids reacted as though Santa had come again, and spent the afternoon playing in the snow. Krisztina helped an unsteady J.J. make his way through the snow, obviously enjoying herself as well.

Mitch and I were stacking wood, just out of earshot of the others so we could rehash possibilities. He was seething with anger as his axe slammed through another log. In silence, I picked up the halves and stacked them. "I knew it," he muttered through clenched teeth. Laying another log on the chopping stump he raised the axe above his head. "They had to have known we were here." The crack of the axe drowned out the word he used to describe the invaders.

I gathered up the wood again. "What bothers me is that there's nothing we can do about it." I looked into Mitch's eyes, trying to read through the anger, wondering if he could see the revulsion I felt.

Slamming the axe into the chopping block he pulled up another log to sit on and reached for a bottle of water. Downing the contents of the souvenir shop bottle, he leaned his elbows onto the large chopping block and hung his head in his hands.

I watched as his shoulders sagged. "You OK?" I put a hand on his shoulder and waited for a response.

The fury that flashed in his eyes when he lifted his head had me take a step back. "No, I'm not OK!" He stood and pointed back and forth between the two of us. "WE are not OK!" His voice had risen so much that Krisztina and the kids turned to see what was going on.

I raised my hands, trying to avert a full blown outburst. "Don't ruin their day," I said in a hushed voice. "They think Santa brought the snowsuits, let's not spoil their fun." I waved off Krisz and turned back to Mitch. It had taken Mitch's accident that night to get him to stop obsessing over the alien's doings and focus on group living. Now I feared we were back at square one. He had that look in his eyes again.

Chapter Nine

Mitch's mood remained dark over the next few weeks and it was beginning to take its toll on group morale. It was well into the night by now and Mitch had not yet returned from his 'excursion'. Krisztina paced in front of the fire as I loaded the hearth with wood. I was beginning to wonder if we would have enough to get through the winter. Pushing the thought from my mind, I turned back to Krisz and gestured for her to join me in front of the fire.

She shook her head and continued to pace as she chewed absently on a finger. "He just makes me so mad. He won't tell us where he's going or when he's coming back. What if something happens to him, seriously, then what?" She paused a moment, clenching her fists at her sides before stepping between me and the fire. "Why didn't you try and talk some sense into him? You're the oldest. We can't risk losing him to some crazy quest."

The sound of Mitch pushing his way through the door nipped her rant in the bud. Avoiding our gazes Mitch quickly undressed and headed for the food shelves to scrounge for something to eat. Dropping into a chair, he proceeded to stuff his mouth with bannock and jam. No one said a word. Most nights, though we were still awake when he came in, we were in bed and avoided confrontation.

Krisztina gestured for me to go talk with Mitch, but I held up a hand, out of Mitch's sight, and mouthed 'no' to her. I'd try and talk with him in the morning. Provoking him now would get us nowhere, and waking the kids would only stress them out.

"What?" Mitch shot at Krisz with a scowl. "If you have something to say to me, then say it." His eyes held hers a moment before he resumed his ravenous attack on the bread.

I stood and stepped between the two. "We were just worried about you, that's all." I reached behind my back for Krisz's arm and ushered her towards her sleeping area. "You were out later than the other nights."

"Jamie was upset that you missed supper," Krisz added from her side of the shelter as she turned her back to us to change.

Mitch grunted, barely turning his head in her direction. I sat down on the chair next to him, carefully choosing my words. I hated when he was in this kind of mood, almost too dangerous to approach, let alone confront. I clasped my hands together and laid them on the table before me. "It isn't funny, Mitch," I said in a low, un-accusing voice. "Jamie thought you had disappeared. He fell asleep in tears tonight." I tilted my head slightly, hoping to see some kind of reaction from him. If I hadn't been watching I would have missed the slight pause and slouch of his shoulders.

He shrugged. "Some things he'll just have to accept."

Krisztina snorted. "Like having a crazy brother," she mumbled.

I shut my eyes, hoping he wouldn't take the bait.

"Whatever," he said, pushing away from the table. Without a second glance he headed off to bed. "Where's Jamie?" His tone was filled with tension.

Letting out an exaggerated sigh Krisz stood to look at him. "He's here." She pointed down towards her feet. "With Ally."

I stopped him from crossing over to his brother. "Leave him. He had a hard enough time falling asleep." My eyes searched his. "Let him rest. He's fine where he is."

Pushing past me he stormed over to his brother's side and dropped down to the floor. His hand shook as he gently stroked Jamie's cheek. I laid a hand on his shoulder, careful not to startle him, and nodded for him to follow me out of Krisz's side of the room.

With a forced sigh he stood and headed back to our side of the room, but not before he shot Krisztina a hard look. Shaking my head and whispering a grateful prayer for Krisztina who held her tongue, I got ready for bed.

* * *

After breakfast, Krisztina took the three kids out for a bit of fresh air. It was cold and they wouldn't be able to stay out for long, but I needed some privacy to talk to Mitch. He sat at the end of the table, arms crossed, with an obstinate look on his face. Offering a silent plea for help I took a seat beside him. I pushed back the food that had been left on the table, drew in a deep breath and turned to face him. "So, what have you learned?" I decided to take the non-confrontational route. "There must be something that keeps calling you back." OK, so maybe I was pushing it a bit. I sat back and waited for the anger in his eyes to dim.

He shook his head and leaned closer. "Doesn't it bother you that they know we're here?" He clenched his jaw.

"Of course it does. But then you are assuming that the clothing came from them. How do you know it wasn't from our own people? Maybe it was all they could do to help for now. The clothes could have come from any store or outlet we would have shopped at." I searched his face for a reaction, but he continued to avoid my gaze. "It's not as though we received strange alien garments."

He closed his eyes. "What about the thing they were wrapped in?" Slowly, he opened his eyes and turned to face me. He looked tired and harried.

I shrugged. "We have no way of knowing since it disappeared. Besides, it's not like we know all our government's technological secrets." I paused and waited, watching him carefully. "Did you find what you were looking for?"

He shook his head. "I didn't find anything." He jammed his hands into his hair. "I don't even know what I'm looking for." A strange emotion crossed his face, giving him an air of torment. "Look, this whole situation is making me crazy, I just…"

Krisztina pushed open the door and stuck her head in. "You almost done? It's getting cold, Jamie's starting to cough and J.J.'s overdue for his nap."

I clenched my jaw, letting out a breath of frustration. Why couldn't she have held on another few minutes? Before I could answer Mitch was dressing to head outside. So much for that… "Just bring them in." There was no sense in letting them freeze.

"Can we get something to eat?" Jamie and Ally charged at me before even bothering to undress. J.J. sat by the door, mercilessly dumped and abandoned by Krisz.

"Let's get you all undressed, put J.J. down for his nap and then we can prepare a snack together." I was grateful for the enthusiastic nods I got. Heading to take care of J.J., I couldn't help but overhear Mitch and Krisz going at it, again. At least they were doing it outside. J.J. was propped up against the wooden wall, eyes closed with his little mouth making a sucking motion. Frowning, I scooped him up and carted him over to his bed. Krisztina was usually so mothering to him, I didn't understand how she could just dump him on the floor.

Jamie and Ally stepped closer as I slipped the little man out of his snowsuit and settled him beneath his blankets. The three of them had glowing cheeks, a testimony to how cold it was outside. Jamie touched my arm cautiously. "Could we choose something from the cans for lunch, please?" he whispered.

Ally twisted on the spot. "Just this time," she pleaded.

I laughed. "Go look through our supplies and pick out what you want." I had barely finished my sentence before they scurried off, giggling. I shook my head. Remembering Mitch and Krisz arguing, I moved closer to the door to listen. Nothing. Opening the door, I took a quick peek, not wanting to disturb their 'conversation'. Neither of them were anywhere to be seen. I listened to see if I could hear them talking but aside from the sounds of the wind that had started to pick up, I couldn't hear them. Now that was strange. Maybe they had decided to continue their discussion somewhere out of ear shot.

After a hardy meal of cartoon-character pasta and a whole pack of chocolate covered cookies, we settled down to practice some reading and writing. Things got a little out of hand when we started singing made up songs, but it was well worth the laughs. J.J. clapped and laughed enthusiastically at their silliness.

Jamie's face turned into a frown mid-song. "When is my brother coming back?" He looked around the room. "I'm hungry."

"You know what?" I asked Jamie. "I'm kind of hungry myself. Let me go see if Mitch and Krisztina are around. Then we can get supper ready." I didn't have a watch so I had no idea how much time had passed since the two had left. "Why don't the two of you tidy up and go pick out something for supper."

The squeals of delight kept the two busy while I slipped out the door to look for our missing group members. I was surprised to be greeted by the darkness of night. I had not realized they'd been gone so long. "Mitch! Krisztina!" I waited for an answer, shivering without a jacket. "Come eat!" A feeling of uneasiness settled in the pit of my stomach. I wasn't sure what had happened, but the unease I felt told me it wasn't good.

"Boy is it cold outside," I commented as I hurried to the fire to warm up. "Hand me some more wood, Jamie."

"You're supposed to say 'please'," Ally interjected.

I smiled, despite the worry I felt. "Right you are, Miss Manners." I turned to Jamie and accepted the piece of wood he brought me. "Thank you, kind sir," I said in an exaggerated tone.

Ally giggled and continued to set the table for our meal.

Just as we were sitting down to eat, Mitch pushed open the door and entered, bringing a gust of wind and snow with him. He looked half frozen as he stripped off his outer-wear and moved in close to the fire.

Exchanging glances around the table, no one said a thing. Even J.J. sat unmoving, staring at Mitch. I stood and dished out some stew for Mitch, walked over to him and handed him the bowl, leaving him to warm himself by the fire. I wanted to know where Krisz was, but I figured asking him in front of the others would only cause them to worry.

Sensing something was off, Jamie and Ally finished up their meal quickly and headed off to the outhouse together while I readied J.J. for bed. The three of them settled on Krisztina's side of the shelter and Jamie offered to read the bedtime story. I gave him a grateful smile and placed the tiny, battery-operated lamp so he could see the book.

Mitch hadn't so much as said a word the whole time I cleaned up. I half listened to Jamie read the story, and then to the sound of their breathing as it changed, one by one, telling me they had fallen asleep. Finally, it was now time for answers.

I moved with determination and took a seat on the makeshift bench facing Mitch. Without saying a word I searched his face, trying to read his expression. I drew in a sharp breath and dove in. "What happened, and where is Krisztina?" I was in no mood to be placated.

Anger flashed in his eyes. "I have no idea where that crazy chick went." The muscles in his jaw bulged. He sprang from his seat and began to pace the floor. "I looked everywhere. She must be hiding or something, I don't know." He jammed his hands through his hair, leaving them on end. "I was sure she'd come back, and that I had been wasting my time searching." His voice cracked.

Not realizing I had been holding my breath, I let it out slowly. Now what? It was dark and there'd be no way to find her.

Grief filled Mitch's eyes, his voice dropped to a whisper. "What if something happened to her?"

I closed my eyes and shook my head slowly, trying to keep from panicking. "Why didn't you come get me?"

"And do what? Drag the kids along with us?" He moved about nervously "I'm half frozen, my clothes are soaked and I wouldn't know where to look for her." He dropped down onto the bench. "We can't just leave her out in the cold."

"Didn't you follow her trail?"

"Look, by the time I realized she wasn't coming back I went after her. As it started getting dark I couldn't find her trail anymore and I was afraid I wouldn't make it back either." He was trembling visibly now.

Bile rose in my throat. The thought of her freezing to death out in the cold terrified me. I'd had such a hard time adjusting to the cold that I couldn't imagine being lost, alone and half-frozen. I prayed she would be safe for now, or at least until we could find her. "What's the plan?"

"I'm out of here at the crack of dawn. I'll bring some extra warmers and food with me." He leaned in closer to the fire and let his shoulders slump.

"What if you need a stretcher or something to bring her back?" The memory of having seen dead people flashed in my mind and I shook it off. She had better not die just because of a moment of stupidity. I braced my hands on my knees and stood up. "Might as well pack up what you'll need right away. Hopefully she'll show up sometime tonight."

Mitch scoffed openly at the notion. "I'll probably end up dragging her back kicking and screaming." It was painfully obvious that he was worried about her.

"I hope you're right."

I awoke to find myself alone. Mitch had already gone and it wasn't even daylight. Frustration bubbled through my entire being. I wanted to scream. I couldn't go after him and leave the kids. I wasn't sure I'd be able to handle everything on my own if he didn't return. Damn him! What was wrong with Mitch and Krisztina?

Crouching before the fire I added extra wood, trying to busy myself with what needed to be done. Anything to keep from thinking would be welcome.

The kids slept soundly so I prepared a hearty root vegetable soup and placed it near the fire to simmer. Breakfast would be ready soon and I had started mending some of the kids' clothing. I would check our remedies next and prepare more cough syrup and what ever else we might be running low on. Jamie was sensitive to the cold weather, and often had a hard time breathing.

Jamie woke in a foul mood. He was probably feeling insecure about his brother being away, and I couldn't blame him since I was a mess myself. The day progressed slowly. Jamie and Ally bickered and whined constantly, scraping at my already raw nerves. "Let's go out for some fresh air while J.J. naps," I suggested. Anything would be better than suffering through the rest of the day like this, I thought. "Let's see if we can work on our quinzhee."

"Our what?" Ally asked.

"The igloo house!" Jamie interjected. "I thought you forgot."

I shook my head and turned to Ally. "Mitch and Jamie started it a few days ago. It was supposed to be a guy thing."

Ally wrinkled her nose. "I saw them. They dug a hole in the ground and filled it up again the next day. *That's* not an igloo."

"Well," I said, feeling amused by her assessment. "Let's just say they covered steps one and two. Now we get to dig out the inside."

I finished zipping her up and turned to make sure Jamie was properly dressed as well. "OK, let's get a move on," I said, pushing them out the door.

Using the short camping spades it only took us an hour to dig out the inside of the small quinzhee. Ally sat back along the far wall and surveyed the room. "It's warm in here."

"You still have to watch for frostbite and hypothermia," I said, thinking more of Mitch and Krisztina. I set a camp light in the middle of the room and lit the mantle then hung it from a horizontal branch through the ceiling.

"Isn't all the heat going to go out the hole in the roof?" Jamie asked.

"We need good air circulation, and I feel better about the light being safely out of J.J.'s reach." I looked at Ally and held her gaze. "And you keep your winter clothes on, understood?"

She crossed her arms, a pout forming on her lips.

"How about if I prepare a snack for the two of you to share in here?" I offered.

"Yeah!" they cried unanimously.

"Sit along the wall, don't touch the light and I'll be back in a minute." I hurried to the shelter and gathered the bag I had prepared earlier when I had come in to check on the still sleeping J.J. and fill the lantern.

It would be getting dark soon and there was still no sign of Mitch or Krisztina. I was beginning to doubt they would return. My chest tightened. I didn't know what to think. Fortunately, today had seemed much warmer than yesterday, but thick clouds had been gathering all day, blocking out the sun, and promising new snow.

We ended up eating supper in the quinzhee, and we discussed the differences between their shelter and an igloo. J.J. seemed content to play with colored balls he pushed around the room while we talked.

"They're not coming back, are they?" Jamie asked, cutting Ally off mid-sentence. His eyes glistened with unshed tears.

"I don't know," I answered honestly. "Mitch went to try and find Krisztina. He's tough, right?" I waited for Jamie to nod. "We just have to trust him."

"I said a prayer last night," Ally offered.

I smiled sympathetically at her. "So did I." I stood and scooped J.J., still holding a big red ball, into my arms. "Let's go get ready for bed. I'll tell you a story tonight."

"What about the light?" Ally asked.

"We can bring it to the outhouse and then I'll shut it off." We had run a small rope from the shelter to the outhouse to avoid using a light after dark and prevent anyone from getting lost. Right now, I didn't care about the *no light at night* rule.

I tucked the three of them in on Krisz's side for the night once again. Ally grabbed my hand as I stood to leave. "Could you stay until we fall asleep?"

I squeezed her hand gently and sat back down. "Sure."

"And could you ask Mitch to come see me if he comes back?"

Jamie asked.

I reached over and smoothed the hair from his forehead. "I promise." I settled back and began to sing an old Croatian lullaby I had heard a nurse-maid sing to the children in the clinic every night. I didn't know exactly what the words meant, but it had seemed to soothe the children on the ward.

"More je sve.

Dalje bes te.

Sunce je zima svaki dan.

Srce na kriz.

Dus a nemir.

Dusico moja spava sam

...sleep well," I whispered as I left the room and headed for yet another peek outside.

* * *

The loud clanking of a bell assaulted my senses, pulling me mercilessly from a dream. I sat up, disorientated, not understanding where the sound could be coming from. Jumping to my feet as reality hit, I pulled on my boots, grabbed my jacket and tore out of the shelter. Heading to the hot spring, the only place we had hung a bell in case of an emergency. I pulled out a small flashlight. That's twice in one day I break the no light rule.

I could see Mitch holding Krisztina afloat in the water. They were both fully dressed. Somehow I didn't think thawing out in hot water was the best or recommended method. Mitch was peeling Krisz's clothing off.

He looked up at me, his eyes red and his cheeks as white as snow. "Get us some blankets," he said through chattering teeth, "and get me another pair of shoes so I can walk back to the shelter."

I hurried back for blankets and the makeshift toboggan he had fashioned for the kids. I grabbed the thermometer from the first aid kit on a hunch. Krisztina had started to move and was moaning. Incoherent, she began struggling against Mitch's support. Placing a layer of blankets on the toboggan, I pulled her out of the water with Mitch's help and folded the covers across her. "Stay in the water, I'll be right back." Dragging the dead weight as fast as I could without her falling off the sled was difficult. I scooped Krisztina up and carried her through the door effortlessly. Months of hard work and manual labor was showing its worth. Gingerly, I laid her in front of the fire where I had been asleep earlier. I wrapped the blankets tight, hoping she wouldn't move until I got back. I turned to leave, then remembered the thermometer and took a reading from her ear canal. 96 degrees…I sighed with open relief. It was not as bad as I had feared. OK, now to get Mitch inside.

Using the sled to haul the wet clothing, was probably more difficult than if I would have had to haul Mitch. Seeing him walking beside me was such a relief. Now to find out what the consequences of their stupidity would be.

I ushered Mitch inside and haphazardly hung the wet clothing on the pegs along the outside wall of our shelter. My fingers were frozen in no time, and I began to shiver uncontrollably. I could not imagine having to spend the night out in the cold. Hurrying inside I slammed the door shut and joined Mitch and Krisz before the fire. Mitch had changed into warmer clothes and was stripping off the rest of Krisztina's wet garments. I grabbed a sweat suit and warm socks to dress her in, but first I needed to check her for injuries.

Except for signs of frostbite on her cheeks, nose and lips, her hands and feet seemed fine. There were no other visible injuries. Once she was dressed I applied a salve to her face, covering the discolored skin. "Where'd you find her?" I didn't turn to face him, but remained focused on the task at hand. When he didn't answer I tilted my head to see why. He sat with his knees bent, elbows propped on top and he was holding his head in his hands. Tears ran down his cheeks.

I sat back on my heels. I can't do this anymore. I stood and went to the pot in the hearth; it still contained some soup. I ladled out a cup for each of us and sat down beside him. "Here, this will help warm you."

He took the offering without a word and slowly sipped from his cup. I wondered if we could get some warm soup into Krisztina, or if we should just leave her. I wished Mom were here.

"I thought she was dead," Mitch's voice was barely audible. He raised a tear streaked face. "She was curled up in a heap in the snow. She had paced along some kind of invisible barrier, I could see her tracks." His voice broke. "I didn't know what to do."

I let out a long breath. "She's safe now. We need to get her warmed up, and hope for the best." I'd ask about the 'invisible barrier' later, but for now I preferred to ignore it.

"You were right, you know." His eyes held a look of despair I had seen before. "It's time to grow up and accept our fate, I guess." He put his empty cup down. "No matter what that might be."

"Look, we can't give up yet. Someone knows we're here, and whether they are our people or not, they did try to help us." I reached for his cup to refill it. "One day at a time, that's all we can do."

"I kept thinking about Jamie, and how I couldn't leave him. I thought I had killed Krisztina, and everything was just so out of hand..." his voice trailed off.

"We're doing the best we can. I don't know how just anybody could survive out here, under these conditions." I turned to check on Krisztina who moaned and started to stir.

Her eyes flickered open. "So thirsty," she managed.

Relief washed through me. "Hold on, I'll get you some warm broth." I ladled out some of the broth from the top of the pot. Mitch supported her shoulders, just enough for her to sip from the cup. "Easy," I said. "Take small sips."

She turned her head away after a sip. "Just water, or tea, please."

Mitch lowered back to the floor, and sat by her side, stroking her hair, talking to her in a low voice while I made tea. When would all this end?

After Krisztina had fallen asleep, Mitch checked in on Jamie, being careful not to wake his brother.

"Why don't you get some sleep," Mitch said, nodding toward our room. "I'm going to stay here by the fire."

I nodded. I wouldn't be more than a few feet away if there was anything. I think the worry had taken more out of me than any of the physical labor had. Not bothering to undress or even climb under my blankets, I fell asleep as soon as I hit the mat.

Chapter Ten

We slept until noon, undisturbed. At one point J.J. must have managed to join me because I awoke to his tiny hands slapping my cheeks. Ally's voice was almost in a panic. "Where is J.J.? I thought you were watching him."

I smiled at J.J. "Busted, my man." I sat up and pulled him close to tickle him, giving away his location. Ally scurried in, obviously with the intention of hushing him, but I raised a hand to cool the fire. "It's OK, I'm awake." I looked down at J.J. "And hungry!" Jamie, by now, would know his brother had made it home safe and sound.

Mitch and Krisz were still asleep, oblivious to what was going on around them. Mitch looked exhausted, but Krisztina was not so lucky. Her face was swollen, and her lips were cracked and had some dried blood on them. At least her color was better than I had expected. She still had a coat of salve on her skin so I decided to let her rest for now.

The smell of food must have gotten through to Mitch, for minutes after I had finished preparing lunch for everyone, he awoke. Krisztina continued to sleep through the day, but we managed to get some liquids into her. I started to reapply the salve while she was half awake, and she whimpered at my touch. "I'm sorry, I know it hurts." I brushed the hair from her eyes. "Try to sleep some more. You'll feel better after a good night's rest."

She nodded weakly and let me settle her back down without protest. Ally watched from behind the table. "Why don't you give me a hand, Ally?"

Cautiously, she moved closer. Her grey-blue eyes were wide as she took a closer look at Krisztina's face. "It hurts, doesn't it?"

I nodded. "She froze her face a bit, but she'll be OK." I held up the jar of salve. "Maybe your touch won't hurt her as much."

Her little hand trembled as she reached out to apply the salve.

She kept looking nervously from Krisz's face to mine. I smiled in reassurance and gestured for her to continue.

Ally jumped back when Krisztina shifted and opened her eyes slightly. "Thank you," Krisztina whispered.

I gave Ally a thumbs up and whispered, "Good job."

She blushed and looked away. I placed a finger under her chin and gently lifted her head so our eyes could meet. "Thank you for your help. You did a better job than I did." I held her gaze. "And thank you for letting us sleep in today."

She threw herself in my arms and gave me a big hug. I kissed the top of her head and hugged her back. My heart swelled in my chest. I really did love our family. I looked over at Mitch and Jamie sitting at the table. Jamie was over the moon that his brother was back, waving his arms as he enthusiastically described how we had finished the quinzhee. I caught Mitch's gaze, and could see how grateful he was to be back with his brother.

The day played out without incident, and once Mitch and I had finished getting the little ones settled for the night, we found ourselves sitting at the table. Now we could discuss what he had seen when he'd found Krisztina. He didn't need any prompting. "We're stuck inside some kind of cage," he said. "I don't know how long Krisz had run back and forth along the perimeter of this thing, but by the time I'd found her all I could think about was getting her back here before she froze to death."

"What exactly do you mean by *cage*?" I clasped my hands together and leaned in a little closer, keeping my voice low. No need to scare the kids.

He passed a hand through his hair. "Like I said, Krisz had more time to check it out, but from what I saw, it's as though we're inside some kind of transparent dome, wall or cage."

I thought about it for a moment. "I'd go with cage or barrier, since we're still getting weather changes, and some birds and insects came back. If it were a dome we'd probably have been cut off."

He grunted, passing a hand over his mouth. "Makes sense."

"Did you touch it?" Part of me would have liked to have seen it.

He nodded. "It was soft and hard at the same time. Kind of like it wasn't really there, but the harder you pushed, the harder it got." He shrugged. "I didn't really take much time to examine it, you know, because of Krisz."

"I'm just glad you got her back in time." I let out a weary breath. How long could we last like this, I wondered. The thrill of adventure had definitely gone stale.

"There's one thing, though." Mitch's voice was shaky. He pressed his lips together and drew in a deep breath before going on. "What if everything inside the barrier is to be destroyed?"

My stomach lurched. I hadn't thought of that. I felt my chest tighten and I had to fight down a wave of panic. Losing control wouldn't do any of us any good. Taking a few breaths to calm myself, I tried to think clearly. "If we consider how long it's taken them to dig out half the city, we should have a few months before they make it here." My mind tried to come up with possibilities. "That's if they even intend to come this far. There were no buildings here and so far they seem to be harvesting the area around the crumbled town."

Mitch tilted his head as he considered my words. "That would give us some time to figure out how to get out of here."

"Winter would be over too, and that'd make things easier." I could not imagine having to try an escape in this weather.

"So what do we do?" Mitch asked.

"I guess all we can do is make it through the winter and then try to find a way beyond the barrier." I had no idea how we could do it, but we'd have plenty of time to figure something out while we waited for the snow to melt. "Could you see on the other side of the barrier?"

He nodded his head slowly. "Yeah, but it was just as wild as it is here."

"Do you think we could focus on the group, on making it through the winter without a repeat of past behavior?" It was worth a try. A little piece of mind until spring hit would be welcome, if he accepted.

"I'm sorry about the attitude. I never thought things would get so out of hand." He really did look sorry. I wasn't sure he would be able to keep his promise, but as long as he tried...

"Let's throw more wood onto the fire and call it a night. We'll need to replenish our wood pile tomorrow. I have a feeling we've got more snow on the way." I stood and stretched. The weight of responsibility had definitely made its mark on my body. I felt worn, tired and very old.

By morning Krisz was running a fever. Great, I thought, I just hope she doesn't come down with pneumonia. I rechecked the thermometer.

"Well?" Mitch asked again. He hadn't come to her side, but he was constantly hovering over me.

I frowned. "She's holding at 102.3"

"Well shouldn't we uncover her and rub her down with alcohol or something?" His brows came down as he scrutinized Krisz's sleeping form. We had moved her back to her side of the shelter, leaving room for the kids to move around. For some reason, they were particularly hyper today.

I couldn't hide my surprise. "Why? Her body is just doing what needs to be done. Why are westerners so afraid of a fever?"

He grabbed my arm. "What if it gets too high?"

I put down the thermometer, mustering the calming tone I had heard Mom use more than once. "That's why I'm keeping an eye on it. If it gets too high I'll give her something to bring it down. For now, there's no cause to worry." I couldn't let him know that not only was I worried, but I wasn't sure if I could handle what was coming. Time to flip through those home remedy books we'd collected. Thank God we had them.

Bickering from Jamie and Ally drew me from my thoughts. We should probably dress the lot of them and wear them out in the snow. I sighed. "There must be something in the air." Mitch rolled his eyes. I stepped from Krisz's side and bit back a smile at his exasperated look. "Time to go play in the snow," I said, then went to check on the pot simmering in the hearth. Lunch would be ready soon. Good timing.

Ally and Jamie hurried to get their snow suits and dropped down on the floor to dress. I grabbed J.J. as he scooted by and got him ready as well. Meanwhile, Mitch was fully dressed and waiting by the door to take them outside. He stopped me as I reached for my jacket. "I'd feel better if you stayed in with Krisz, just in case."

"Oh, OK. I wanted to look up a few things anyway." I gave him a once over. "Are you sure?"

"Yeah, I'm sure." He nodded towards the kids. "I can handle

them."

I couldn't help but notice how overdressed he was. OK, it wasn't funny. I guess he was afraid of getting cold again. Stepping over to the door to pull it shut, my attention was drawn to the dark charcoal clouds in the sky. Wow, we were going to get it bad. Huge snowflakes swirled around on gusts of wind. This was going to be a short play period.

"Hey," Ally yelled out, pointing to the sky. "Did you see that?"

"I didn't see anything," Jamie said.

"Lightning! I saw lightning," she insisted.

I looked at Mitch who was still holding on to J.J. "Lightning, in the winter?" I asked. "Is that possible?"

He puffed his cheeks as he let out a breath. "Yeah, and if I'm not mistaken, it means we're going to get a lot of snow."

I shook my head in despair. "I guess we'll know soon enough. Wear them out, I'll be right here." I pulled the door shut and went to reload the fireplace.

Within half an hour the group was pounding on the door with a load of firewood. Mitch had everyone working to replenish our indoor supply. I pulled in the toboggan and quickly unloaded the wood to our pile, then shoved the toboggan back out again. One more load and we'd be good for days.

The entire group entered with the second load, covered in snow and looking a little tired. Well, that's one way to wear them out. I turned away to hide my amused look, pretending to check on lunch. "Who's hungry?" I asked. Frowning at the lack of response, I turned back and saw that if we didn't get some food into them soon, they'd fall asleep on empty stomachs. "Jamie, come help me dish out lunch. Ally, get J.J. out of his clothes and settled at the table, OK?"

She nodded and moved to care for her brother. Mitch took care of the wood on his own. "How is she?" he asked as he tossed the logs atop the pile.

"No change in temp." I paused a moment to consider her condition. "Hopefully it won't be more than a bad cold. If we're lucky she'll be fine once the fever breaks." She had started coughing and her chest was definitely congested. We'd know soon enough.

"I suppose we're lucky then if that's the worst of it." He shoved the toboggan out the door and closed it, but not before a gust of wind sent a swirl of large snowflakes across the room.

"That doesn't look good," I said.

Mitch snorted. "It's going to get a whole lot worse."

"Great," I said, my tone dripping with sarcasm. "Well, let's eat." I took one of the books we had found at the gift shop to the table. It covered all kinds of strange facts about Montana, including snowfall.

"Wait," Jamie called out as Mitch was about to spoon food into his mouth. "We didn't say Grace. You promised." He eyed his brother with determination.

Mitch lowered his spoon and reached out to ruffle his brother's hair, giving him a half smile. Everyone held hands and Jamie gave thanks. Mitch leaned closer to me and mumbled. "We did this back home, and he said he'd promised to not forget to give thanks if I came back."

I pressed my lips together and shrugged. "Small price to pay for a miracle."

Mitch threw me a strange look, then turned his attention to his food and dug in.

I opened the book and read out some of the facts. "Did you know that Montana is one of the few places where lightning can be seen in the winter? And that it usually means a lot of snow is coming." I looked up at Mitch. "You get an average snowfall of 300 inches in a Montana winter?" I didn't believe it.

He shook his head. "Not so much in the city." Tearing a piece of bannock he added with a wry grin, "but then, we're not in the city."

The look of horror on my face seemed to amuse him.

"Relax," he said. "It doesn't come down all at once." He laughed, winking at Jamie.

After supper I continued to prepare remedies for Krisztina. Spread across the table, I had jars, honey, garlic and herbs we'd grown, along with the essential oils I had taken from the store. The usual wood smoke smell of our shelter was replaced with the distinct smell of eucalyptus, and other herbs as I mixed batches of everything from cough syrup to a chest rub. Mitch sat down next to me and watched as I mixed the last batch. He pointed to the books on the table. "All these things are in those books?"

I shook my head. "No, I've made some of these before. My mother used to have me prepare batches of the simple remedies." I looked around the room. "You get the kids down already?"

He nodded vigorously. "They were exhausted."

I let out a slow breath. "You and Krisz being gone took its toll on them."

"Yeah," he admitted, then paused before adding, "I actually felt like I'd come home when I saw our shelter."

I tilted my head as I thought about that. "On some level, we're lucky to have this place to live in. You know, compared to how I've seen other people live."

Mitch held my gaze. "Don't worry, I realized that over the past two days."

"So, why do you obsess over things you can't change?" I avoided his gaze, hoping I wouldn't set him off, but it was a behavior I couldn't seem to grasp.

He shrugged. "Maybe you don't understand because of how you grew up, but injustice makes me so mad." The muscles in his jaw tightened. "I mean, come on, someone knows we're here, but instead of helping, they just leave us to fend for ourselves."

"We shouldn't get so worked up until we have all the facts. Trust me, I have seen injustice first hand, and more pain and suffering to last several lifetimes, but you're missing the point," I tried to find a way to put it into words. "Injustice really makes me angry, but being angry isn't productive and it's a waste of energy. In any given situation you have to do what you can, no matter how small a gesture. We can't afford to waste effort on things we can't change." I paused, giving him time to absorb my talk. Wow, I was beginning to sound like my parents. I decided to go for broke. "You know, being angry or frustrated is like a rocking chair. It won't get you anywhere, but it'll give you something to do." I watched his expression change.

He laughed under his breath and punched me in the shoulder. "You can be so strange."

We sat in silence for a while, lost in thought. The room was filled with the rhythmic sound of slow breathing and the crackling fire, interrupted only by the occasional gust of wind outside.

Krisztina's coughing fit snapped us out of our lull. Rubbing my eyes I stood and gathered the syrup and salve, heading to her side.

"Mitch, could you boil water and add it to that cup?" I nodded to the big mug on the table. "I have already added the herbal mixture in a little pouch for her."

Krisztina was on her side, coughing. Tears ran from her eyes as she tried to cough into her bunched-up cover. I moved to her side and lifted her head and shoulders, holding her until the fit passed. Wiping her eyes with the damp cloth from the nearby tray, I spoke softly to her, trying to calm her. She was a sight, with matted hair and a puffy face. Leaning heavily on me, she tried to clear some of the congestion from her lungs. "Here, take this." I held out a spoonful of syrup. "It'll help, trust me, and the taste is not that bad."

She opened her mouth and took it, still leaning on me. I caught Mitch's worried expression as he joined us, holding the steaming brew. "It's too hot," he said.

I nodded. "It'll cool off soon enough." I pointed to the jar of salve. "Hand that to me, will you?" I shifted Krisz slightly so I could have access to her back. "I'm going to rub some salve on your back," I told her. "It'll soothe your muscles and help you breathe a little easier."

She nodded, not resisting my touch. Mitch knelt close, holding the open jar. His nose and brow wrinkled as he caught a whiff of the salve. He just looked at me, eyes watering. Ignoring him, I rubbed the paste into Krisz's back, massaging her muscles at the same time. "I'm going to lie you back down and put some on your chest and neck."

She stiffened momentarily, but let herself be guided down to her bedding. I applied some salve to her neck and upper chest.

Mitch held out the cup and straw. I nodded. "I'm going to go wash my hands. Why don't you try to give her some?"

He nodded and moved in closer. I could hear him talking softly as I headed for the table to clean up my mess. Once I had restored the jars to their place, I dressed and went outside before heading to bed. The wind had picked up and heavy snow engulfed me. Holding the safety rope, I made my way out, blinded by a squall. The kids would have to use the portable potty tonight. I don't think we'd be going back out until this was over.

Mitch was waiting for me with a mug of warm cocoa when I got back. "Looks bad out there," he said.

I shook off the snow and hung up my coat. "Now that's an understatement." I accepted the mug and sat beside him, staring at the fire.

"She fell asleep," he said. "She seems to be breathing easier, too."

I nodded, relieved that the mixture had worked. "Thank God."

"I checked on the kids, they're all sleeping soundly," Mitch said, focused on his cup. "It's so weird, isn't it?"

I lifted my head to face him. "What is?" I had no idea what he was talking about. If you asked me, there wasn't much about our situation that wasn't 'weird'.

"How close we all are." He put his cup down, an expression of contemplation on his face. "Jamie is my little brother, but I think I feel just as protective of everyone else." He sighed. "When I think of us getting out of this mess, the only thing that scares me is losing sight of one another."

I smiled half-heartedly. "I know what you mean." I swallowed back the lump forming in my throat. I had never felt this close to anyone before, not even my parents. Maybe it was because everyone else had always seemed to come first. "We'll just have to find a way to keep in touch." If ever we do get out of here, I thought to myself.

Mitch stood and collected our cups. "Time to get some sleep." He stretched and yawned. "Our family is going to need a bath tomorrow. Maybe after we finish shoveling all this snow we could take them into the hot spring, rather than haul water here."

Now that would be interesting. "OK, I'm game. You go crash with the kids," I nodded to our side of the room. "I'll sleep next to Krisz. She'll probably wake up often."

He nodded, shoulders sagging with fatigue, and headed for bed. "Well, good night then."

"Good night." I rose to collect the syrup and salve, changed the damp cloth and poured more hot water over the herbal mix. It would probably be a long night, but at least this time everyone was home. I settled with my back against the half wall and watched Krisztina sleep. At some point, sleep claimed me as well.

I lost count of the number of times I had to care for Krisz throughout the night, but by morning I was exhausted. It felt as though my insides were shaking. At least now I could get some sleep while Mitch cared for her and the kids.

The room was eerily quiet, except for the sound of the others breathing in a slow, rhythmic manner. The fire had burned down to a bed of coals so I added more wood. Wanting a bit of fresh air I headed to the door, just for a peek at the new snow, but the door was stuck. My heart rate kicked up a notch and I braced myself against the wall and pulled with all my might. Slowly, the door opened an inch. Mustering my strength, I pushed with my legs and pulled hard and steady. The door opened…to a wall of snow. The wind must have blown the snow up against our shelter. The ledge we had settled under had seemed to be a good idea at the time, keeping rain off us…but it must have caught the snow in the wind and packed it down on us. We were snowed in. I could barely breathe as I thought about those three-hundred inches of snow. When would this end?

Chapter Eleven

My chest tightened and I felt like I was going to hyperventilate. I had never been in this kind of situation. This had to be someone's idea of a sick joke. Forcing some slow breaths I hurried to wake Mitch. Better he saw this before the others woke up. We had left the shovels out by the quinzhee. Now what were we going to do?

Mitch sat up groggily, but as soon as his eyes focused on my face he jumped up and practically dragged me from the room. "What's wrong? Is she OK?" he asked.

I nodded. Moving shakily to the door, I pointed. "I think we have a problem." With a grunt I pulled the door open.

"Shit!" He moved to touch the wall of snow. "How deep is it?"

"How the heck should I know? What are we going to do now?" I pulled at my shirt collar, hoping to relieve the choking feeling. My insides were shaking again.

Mitch closed the door and began to pace in circles, mumbling under his breath. "Shovels outside?"

I felt my cheeks turn red as I nodded. "Up against the quinzhee."

He continued to pace for a moment then stopped dead. "Get me a broom."

"You want to sweep away the snow?" I couldn't wrap my mind around what he wanted the broom for.

He took hold of my shoulders. "Get me a broom, please."

I opened my mouth to say something, but then turned to get the broom. "Here." I watched as he shoved the handle through the snow. He repeated the procedure at intervals from floor to ceiling. Near the ceiling he pushed it upward through the snow. "What are you looking for?" It's not like the broom told him how deep the snow was.

"Daylight." He closed the door and made his way to the fireplace. "I need to think about this." He sat down and rested his head in his hands.

"I'll go check on Krisz." I set the kettle to boil on the single butane round and quietly peeked in to see how she was doing. Her bedding was completely soaked, but she was still sound asleep. I went back to Mitch who hadn't moved from his thinking position.

He tilted his head toward me. "So?"

"The fever broke, but she's soaked. I draped another blanket on her so she doesn't get cold. She'd probably be more comfortable dry but I didn't want to wake her." I pulled out some cups and placed them on the table. "Do you want tea, coffee or cocoa?"

"I could really go for some bacon and eggs," he said in all seriousness.

I laughed, not expecting that for an answer. "I'm sure. So?"

"Whatever you're having." He waved me off. "I have to figure this out."

Since I was so freaked out by our situation, and doing everything *not* to think about it, I'd let him try and solve it. I busied myself preparing breakfast for everyone, hoping to be ready for when they woke up.

"Where's that mirror on a stick?" Mitch asked from his seat. He wasn't focusing on anything in particular as he chewed on his lower lip.

I put down the batter I had been preparing and rummaged around the shelves we'd made along the half-wall. Found it. We had attached the mirror to the stick to look into bird nests so Jamie and Ally could watch the baby birds. "Here." I held it out to him then headed to the fire to add more wood.

"No, wait." Mitch rose and moved close to the fireplace. Using a stick he pushed the coals off to the side. Sliding the mirror into the hearth, he tried to get a peek up the chimney.

"See anything?" I asked, leaning over his shoulder.

He moved out of the way and pointed to the mirror. "What does that look like to you?"

I shrugged. "The inside of the chimney." I had no idea what he wanted as an answer.

He let out an exasperated breath. "Look as far up the chimney as possible."

I made a face before leaning into the still hot fireplace. "I see the chimney, daylight..." Oh, no. Now I know what he saw. "Is it my imagination or has our chimney grown in height?" My head started to spin.

"We're in big trouble." Mitch's voice faltered. "Are you feeling dizzy or light headed?" His tone was serious.

I shrugged. "Just nerves, I guess."

"Go check on the kids, see if you can wake them." He grabbed the boiling water and threw it over the fire.

"What are you doing? We'll freeze!" He must be losing his mind.

"Go check on the others now!"

I jumped back. He had never directed his anger towards me before. I moved quickly to the kid's bedside. Shaking both Jamie and Ally's shoulders at the same time I spoke softly to draw them from their sleep. They didn't respond. I gripped Jamie's shoulders with both hands and shook him. His breathing was shallow and he had a slow steady pulse, but he was totally unresponsive. "What's wrong with them?"

Mitch stepped in and scooped up a child in each arm. "Bring J.J."

I followed suit and lay J.J. on the floor beside the fireplace. A cold draft could be felt pouring in from the chimney. I watched as Mitch rubbed Jamie's arms and legs, roughly stimulating him. He moved on to Ally and nodded for me to do the same with J.J.

I felt sick. They were lacking oxygen. Before I could let my imagination run away with me J.J. coughed and started to cry.

The other two followed suit. Mitch stood and went to get a bowl. "Dress them all very warm and stay back," he said sternly.

"What about Krisztina?" I found my arms full with three crying, sluggish children.

"Dress the kids to keep them warm, put them in back with some food and then tend to Krisz." He yanked open the door and began scooping snow, tossing it along the wall, filling our shelter with snow.

I hadn't finished preparing breakfast, and now there was no longer a fire. *OK, Aleksei, get a grip.* My insides shook as I tried to think of something to feed the kids.

Mitch stopped to stare at me. "Just give them some prepackaged fruit snack or something. Give them chocolate, I don't care." He tossed his arms up in the air and turned away from me.

I scooped up J.J. and put him back in his bed with an extra blanket. Bending down for Jamie I noticed that he'd wet himself. Taking a steadying breath I turned back to the task at hand. OK, I thought to myself, I can do this. It felt as though my mind was in another time zone as I picked up Ally and put her on the camping potty; then turned to strip down Jamie.

The three kids were wailing now, and Jamie was shivering uncontrollably. "I'm going as fast as I can," I said as I pulled a sweatshirt over his head. Ally, still in her pajamas, sat down beside me and slid her legs into her snowsuit. I shot her a grateful smile, wiping the tears from her cheeks. "Do you think you can handle J.J.?" I asked. This would allow me to check on Krisz.

Ally took her brother's clothes and headed over to his bed. I shifted my attention back to Jamie as he sat up and passed a sleeve across his face, smearing all kinds of stuff on it before I had the chance to give him something to wipe his nose. Nice.

Sitting back on my heels I thought a moment. Leaning in so only Jamie could hear, I made him an offer, "If you hurry and dress, I'll let you pick out something for breakfast."

He grumpily slid his feet into his snowsuit, giving me the chance to check on Krisztina. Unlike the kids who had been unresponsive, she was only asleep. Well, maybe it was too deep a sleep to be natural, but she roused when I touched her.

"Why is it so cold," she asked, her teeth starting to chatter.

"Your fever broke," I said in Mom's soothing tone. "You are soaked and in desperate need of a change."

She yanked the covers up under her chin. "Don't even think about it," she snapped.

Oh yeah, she was on the mend. "Can you change or do you need help?" I laid her winter clothes on the edge of the half-wall. "It's going to get a whole lot colder before we can make another fire, so you have to change."

She sat up, holding the covers close to her body with her elbows as she rested her head in her hands. "I feel like I was thrown off a cliff."

I dropped down on one knee beside her and gently laid a hand on her knee. "Do you need help?" She tilted her head and made a face. "Change into the essentials, and I'll help you with the rest."

She let the covers slide and realized she was wearing Mitch's shirt. Her eyes became slits. "You saw me naked!" she hissed.

With a brief shake of my head I stood, ignoring her comment. "Hurry and change, you're going to freeze in those wet covers." I left her alone and stepped onto the other side of the shelter where apparently a party had broken out. Juice boxes, fruit snacks, granola bars and chocolate covered raisins covered the area. Jamie was rummaging around for more items and froze when he saw me standing behind him. I raised an eyebrow and he put the boxes he was holding back. "Good decision," I said. "I think you have more than enough to work with here." I surveyed the mess. "Clean this up, now. I have to help Mitch." I turned on my heel and left to grab an extra sweatshirt; it was really getting cold.

Mitch and I worked for another two hours, piling more and more snow inside our shelter. I used a small propane heater to keep the temperature above freezing, and to keep the chimney tunnel from collapsing. Well, I hoped it would. Mitch's hair was plastered to his forehead and his body gave off steam as he worked. He hadn't even taken a five-minute break since he'd started digging. I had to force him to down a few sips of water. Krisztina and Ally kept the boys busy and out from underfoot, but if we didn't get out soon, we'd freeze or die of asphyxiation.

Mitch slid out of the tunnel he'd been digging and pushed me up into it, pointing. "Daylight," he mouthed barely loud enough for me to hear.

My heart started pounding, our prayers had been answered! I crawled ahead, excited and determined to punch out, but as I made my way to the glimmer of light a thunderous sound filled my ears and the next thing I knew I was trapped. I couldn't move anything above my knees, and even that was limited. From far away I could hear Mitch yelling.

My head rested in the crook of my arm, forming a slight air pocket. The snow was packed tightly around my chest and held me firmly in place, making it impossible to take a deep breath. I had to resort to breathing with my mouth open. The cold took hold through my damp clothing and I began to tremble. Any shred of hope I had left about getting out of this survival situation alive disappeared.

Someone was digging around my knees, but it seemed that every time they loosened the snow around me, it caved back in. I had no idea how long I was stuck there. Things began to get fuzzy, but at least I had stopped trembling. I must have been getting closer to death, because I found myself engulfed in a bright, white light.

I could hear voices but I couldn't understand what they were saying. I still couldn't move, and the bright light was gone. I felt so cold, so empty. Somehow I seemed detached from my body, suspended in time and space. I wasn't sure if the sharp pain in my arm was real or not. I laughed. It felt as though liquid fire was moving slowly through my veins, but it didn't matter. It was probably just a dream.

The next thing I knew, I was walking towards the shelter. Someone had been thoughtful enough to dig out the front and dust the snow off the face of the cliff our shelter was nested in. The path to the outhouse had been neatly shoveled as well. That was nice of them. I didn't see anyone around. Since a steady column of smoke rose from the chimney, I guessed they were all inside.

When I made it to the door, whoever was on my right reached out to open it. There was something familiar about the blue clothing he was wearing, but I couldn't quite remember where I had seen it before. Oh well, no worries.

Everyone was sitting quietly at the table, practically unmoving. Strange, they seemed a little on edge. I'd have to ask Mitch about it later, but now I needed to sit down. I felt myself guided to a chair, then I realized that whoever had been holding me up let go. Mitch still didn't look up. "You OK?" I tried to ask, but my throat was dry and almost no sound came out. This was one strange dream.

The sound of J.J. crying grew louder. I shook off the numbness and cleared my head. Something wasn't right. I stood shakily and made my way to the bed where J.J. stood fussing. I bent down to pick him up and the rush of blood to my head hit like a migraine. "Here, why don't you walk around a bit?" I set him down on the floor to explore his surroundings.

Mitch moaned loudly. I turned to see him holding his head with both hands, leaning heavily on the table. I knew how he felt. Feeling suddenly thirsty I took the glass of water that sat at my place on the table. It had a tangy orange flavor to it, which was surprisingly good. My head cleared instantly. My thoughts became coherent, and the memory of what had happened came back full force. I placed a hand on Mitch's shoulder and offered him his glass when he looked up. He shook his head but I insisted.

Going around the table I got the others to drink up. It was like throwing the power switch on and watching the lot of them come to life.

Mitch studied the others for a moment. When he turned back to me he had a strange look on his face. "We need to talk," he said, uncertainty in his hazel eyes.

I nodded. "Let's send the others outside to play. I could be wrong, but they don't seem to remember anything."

He shook his head. "It happened too fast and they were sitting in back with Krisz. They didn't see a thing. When those guys slipped in everything froze, it was almost like being in some weird dream."

I tried to remember what they looked like. They had stayed strategically out of my field of vision, and when they did pass before my eyes, they had masks or helmets on. "Did you get a good look at them?"

He shook his head. "No more than before. They moved me out of the way and turned me away from what they were doing…" his voice trailed off. He cleared his throat. "What did they do to you?"

I frowned, looking off in the distance as I tried to recall the events of the day. "I remember going up the tunnel to try and punch out. I was excited about the daylight I could see coming through the snow." I passed a hand trough my hair. "I remember a loud rumble and then feeling trapped, crushed and cold."

"Aleksei," Mitch's voice was low, hesitant. "Were you scared?" His eyes studied mine.

I shook my head. "I don't think I had time to be scared, but I do remember thinking it was the end." I shifted my gaze to the floor and suppressed a shudder. I drew in a deep breath then tilted my head toward Mitch. "Did you see the white light?" I asked.

He nodded, eyes wide. "That's when everything kind of went into ultra-slow motion."

Ah, that made sense. I had felt something of the sort myself. Remembering the pain in my arm I rubbed it absently, then pushed up my sleeve and stared at the puncture marks. A little bit of dried blood remained on the inside of my forearm. What exactly had they done to me?

I jumped at Mitch's touch. He turned my wrist over to examine it himself. His eyes searched mine. Swallowing hard I realized Mitch had been right all along. They were watching us, and had been watching us...but why? My stomach turned as my mind came to the sickening realization that we were probably nothing more than some sort of lab experiment or entertainment.

Chapter Twelve

A week later, Mitch, Krisztina and I sat together around the table. The kids slept soundly after having spent most of their day playing outside. Now it was time to talk to Krisz about what had been eating away at both Mitch and me.

She toyed with her empty glass. "I know you want to talk to me about something," she said, not looking at either of us. "You've been acting weird all week."

"Yeah," Mitch replied, shooting me a glance and prompting me to do it.

I closed my eyes and shook my head. Coward. "Do you remember the other day, when it was really cold in here?"

She half shrugged. "The fire went out and you had a hard time getting it going again...so what?"

Dropping my head to hide the look of surprise that crossed my face, I took a steadying breath and composed myself before Krisz could notice. Mitch gave me a 'don't ask me' look.

Krisz continued, "It was cold, but you guys got the situation back in hand, no big deal. Why?" She finally looked up with a hint of amusement on her face. "You macho men feel like you let the women and children down?" She snickered.

My mouth dropped. I sat up, regaining my composure. "No, look we wanted to talk to you about-"

Mitch kicked me under the table and my breath caught in my chest. "Look, we just feel bad," Mitch cut in. "You know, about not doing our job. It did get pretty cold in here."

Krisztina became serious. "Yeah, but you did find me and somehow managed to get me back home..." her voice trailed off as she swallowed back tears. "Thank you for caring enough to do that." She avoided looking at us, again.

J.J. cried out in his sleep and Krisz jumped at the chance to go check on him. I leaned closer to Mitch, shooting a glance to make sure Krisz wasn't paying attention to us. "What do we do?" I asked him. "Do we tell her?" Now I was confused. Did she need to be told what was going on or did we protect her from the truth?

Passing his hand across his mouth, Mitch shook his head with uncertainty. It was as though he had read my mind. "We have to tell her. She has to be in on this with us."

I nodded. "OK." He was right of course.

Plopping back down in the chair next to Mitch, Krisztina grabbed her glass of water and downed it. She looked at the empty glass and made a face.

"Something wrong?" Mitch asked.

She shrugged it off. "No, it's just that for a second I expected it to taste like orange."

Exchanging glances with Mitch made it clear that he wanted me to tell her. "That's because the water they gave us to bring us out of our suspended state tasted like orange." Well, that's one way of jarring her memory.

Krisz made a face. "*What* are you talking about, Aleksei?" Her face changed and she dropped her glass, bringing her hand up to cover her mouth. She started to stand, but Mitch grabbed her arm and gave her a reassuring nod. "It wasn't a dream," she whispered.

I pressed my lips together, shaking my head slowly. "No. They are the ones that dug us out." I took a sip from my glass. I could imagine the orange taste too.

She nodded slowly, and shot a glance toward the door. "Mitch was piling snow inside, trying to clear a path from the door…" She looked off into space. "There was a white light, and then we were just sitting around the table." She shuddered. "I can't remember any details, I'm sorry."

"We're not asking you to," Mitch clarified. "We just want you to realize that they know we're here, and that they've probably known all along."

We sat in silence for a long moment, each lost in our own thoughts. Krisz was the first to speak up. "Then why don't they just let us go?"

I glanced up at Mitch. His nostrils flared with anger and I could see the muscles in his jaw tighten. "Go where?" he asked. "We don't know if the whole planet is like this. We don't know what they did with the others. We don't know what they want or even why they're here." He spat the last bit out through clenched teeth.

Krisztina just stared at him, blinking. "Everything seems fine across the barrier." She touched her fingers to her temple, as though she was calling up a vision. "I walked along it for so long. I'm sure I even saw smoke from a chimney coming from the other side of the ridge."

Mitch pulled his chair closer to the table and clasped his hands in front of him. "That could have been steam from another hot spring."

"No," she shook her head adamantly. "I could smell the smoke." She appeared to be reaching for a memory, just beyond her grasp. "You're wrong about them. They mean us no harm."

Now Mitch and I just stared at each other. Where was that coming from? "They did help us get out of the snow," I admitted.

"And they could have just as easily deposited us somewhere else." He waved an arm to encompass the room. "Somewhere safe and away from this future quarry."

I held up a hand. "We need to decide what we want to do."

Mitch made a gesture to brush me off and let his arm fall on the top of his head. "There's not much we can do," he said with disgust.

I let out a long breath. "Look, at least we know they'll bail us out of any serious trouble for now." I shifted in my seat. "We figure the quarry won't reach us before summer, giving us time to figure out how to get across the barrier. If animals have found a way, so can we."

Mitch grunted. "I guess. But what do we do in the mean time?"

Krisz shrugged. "The only thing we can do. Just keep on doing what we're doing and take things one day at a time."

She was right, at least on some level. I pushed back from the table and stood. "We should get some sleep. I can't remember the last time we had an uninterrupted night."

"Maybe we can get them to deliver some bacon and eggs," Mitch said, soliciting laughs from the three of us.

"We could stamp out the request in the snow," I said jokingly.

"Yeah," Krisz added, "then we'll really know how much they're watching."

I made a face. "Right now, I don't want to know. I think we already know too much and this is definitely one topic where ignorance would be bliss."

Mitch slapped me on the shoulder. "Aw, now where's your sense of adventure?"

I shot him a sideways glance. "Trust me; I've had just about all the adventure I can take. I have officially surpassed my quota for this lifetime."

"Good night," Krisz said, dropping down behind her wall.

"Night." Mitch echoed back. "See you in the morning." He shrugged off his shirt and crawled under his covers wearing his sweats. "You coming?" he asked me.

"Yeah." I pulled my blankets tight around me, but couldn't seem to relax. What if they were watching, even now? They had been inside our shelter…in our personal space, and that knowledge didn't sit well with me at all. I don't know how I was going to go on with routine until the time came to make it out of here. On some level, I understood Mitch's anger and outrage. I just wish there was something we could do about it.

Somehow, amidst my tormented thoughts, sleep managed to claim me.

Even though we all had our first uninterrupted night's sleep in a while, morning still came too fast. As much as I had protested the night before about pretending and going on in a normal fashion until spring came, I soon realized that with three children running around, routine was a necessary evil.

For the first few weeks, we kept close to the shelter, focusing on the kids and their education. I smiled as I thought about the teaching games we had played yesterday. It brought a whole new meaning to 'homeschooling-unschooling'. Our everyday living was a learning experience. But I couldn't help but notice that Mitch had started to wander again, heading back to where he had found Krisztina. When I had asked him about his excursions, he just said he was keeping in shape, hiking and jogging along his now beaten path. I knew he was lying. I knew there was much more to it than he let on, and like so many things in our present situation, there wasn't a thing I could do about it.

I watched as Mitch dressed for the cold while Ally and Jamie played with clay. "Going for a run?" I asked nonchalantly.

He froze for the briefest moment before he turned to face me. "Yeah, I'm working on my endurance. I can run twice the distance

I could when I started."

"I don't doubt it," I said dryly.

"Shh," Krisztina hushed us from her side of the shelter. She was trying to get J.J. down for his nap.

"You two keep playing quietly," I said to our junior sculptors. "I'll be back in a minute to fix us a snack."

Eyes bright, they nodded with enthusiasm.

I grabbed my coat and followed Mitch outside, and out of earshot. The sky was a brilliant blue on this wonderful March day, and the promise of spring was in the air. I filled my lungs with fresh air, and a dose of courage before turning to face him. "What have you found so far?"

The look of surprise on his face betrayed him. "How'd you know?"

I rolled my eyes. "Seriously?" I asked him with a snort. "This is obsessive compulsive behavior on your part."

He took a stance and placed his hands on his hips, pursing his lips. "What do you want me to say?"

"I don't know, how about the truth? Like where you're going and what you're doing." I shook my head in disgust. "Did you really think we didn't know?"

His head dropped and he let out a sigh.

"And you had promised," I added, looking past him.

"I found them," he said, not looking up.

My hand shot out and I gripped his arm. He lifted his head so our eyes could meet. "What do you mean, 'you found them'?"

He nodded slowly. "I found their outpost. I hide along the rocky ledge and watch them."

Oh my God. I closed my eyes and placed a hand on my forehead. I didn't know what to think about that. Taking a steadying breath, I searched his face for signs of dementia. "Are you serious? And you don't think they know you're there? Really?" I turned away in disgust. When all this is over, I'm so looking forward to a little down time on mission somewhere with my parents.

He shifted his weight and kicked a piece of snow with his foot. "You think they know?"

Closing my eyes again, I nodded. Inhaling a steadying breath, my eyes opened slowly, letting his face come into focus. "Come on, Mitch. How long did it take them to show up after I got stuck in the snow?" I shifted my weight. "What about Krisztina? How do you know they hadn't stepped in to keep her alive until you found her?"

I watched as he struggled with the possibilities. "No, that can't be…" his voice trailed off.

I held him in my gaze. "Do you really think that?" I pulled my jacket closed, getting ready to drop the subject. For now. He'd need time to work it out. I started to turn back towards our shelter; then stopped. "How long are you going to be gone this time?"

He danced on the spot. "Look, as much as I may appear to be obsessed with them, I really do need to run and burn off steam." He sighed with a hint of frustration. "Who says two can't play at their game. Maybe they are so sure about themselves that they don't know I'm watching them."

He had a point. Curiosity rose within me. "Have you seen them?"

He nodded. "There are three of them in that thing of theirs."

I furrowed my brows. "What do you mean 'thing'? What does it look like?"

"Like a really bad fort made out of sheets of Styrofoam, just leaning up against one another." He gestured with his hands.

"And you've seen them come and go?" I might take a hike out there with him.

He nodded. "All the time. Either they really don't know that I'm watching, or they don't care."

"Have you seen them without their helmet, or mask?" Not that I really wanted to see what they looked like.

Shaking his head 'no' he started jumping up and down. "Look, I need to get moving. I won't be long, I promise." He shot me one of his more charming grins, but I wasn't convinced.

I held my hands up in surrender. "Fine, go, but just stay out of trouble, and don't come back too late. Jamie gets worried."

Still smiling he shook his head, amused. "Yes, Mom." He didn't need anymore prompting. A second later he was off and running.

I had a bad feeling about this. Oh, how I hated those feelings. I pushed open the door and entered the shelter. Greeted by the comforting smell of a wood fire, and the cocoa Krisz had prepared, this place really did feel like home. In all honesty, this was the first time any place had ever felt this much like home.

"He go running?" Krisz asked.

I nodded, still feeling the knot in my stomach.

She shook her head in disapproval, then handed me a cup of cocoa. "Come see what they're working on," she said with a smile. It showed she was proud of them.

Moving to the table, I leaned over it to examine the mock up the kids had been working on. "Wow, this is really great!" I reached out and gently touched the tiny shelter they had been working on.

Jamie pointed to the side of the shelter where clumps of clay resembled rocks. "Touch." He pointed to the hole in the rocks. "Water."

I nodded in approval. "Good job. This is wonderful. I hope you keep working on it."

"We will," Ally said. "Krisz is going to help us make the fireplace with twigs tomorrow."

I looked up and smiled at her. She blushed.

"Ok, time to put all this away," Krisz cut in. "We have to start on supper, if we plan on eating tonight."

Jamie made a face. "Can't we just open a can?"

Krisz smiled mischievously. "Actually, we'll be opening several cans." She set a can of mushrooms on the table.

"Gross," said Ally, wrinkling her nose. "I'd rather eat Aleksei's strange food."

I faked a hurt look. "Thanks a lot."

Krisz turned back to her bag of supplies, laying out cans of tomatoes and mushrooms, tomato sauce and carrots while the kids watched in silence. Going for dramatic effect, she slowly lifted a plastic container of Romano cheese and a package of spaghetti from her bag.

"Spaghetti!" Jamie called out. "Let's get going, we haven't got all day." He removed the leftover clay from the table and pushed the crumbs to the floor.

I felt a grin creep into my face, lighting my eyes. "Looks like a winner of a meal plan. Do you need my help?"

She shook her head, coordinating her two workers as she waved me off.

I grabbed a book from the shelf and settled down in front of the fire to read. I needed to find myself lost in another world, just to keep my mind off Mitch.

Supper was a success. The kids ate more than I had ever seen them eat since we'd been together. At least they'd sleep well on full bellies. I leaned down to tuck Jamie in. His eyes were heavy with sleep, but it wasn't enough to hide the worry. I leaned down and gave him a kiss on the forehead. "Try not to worry," I said. "He always comes back." I forced a smile as I stood, but the truth was, I was furious with Mitch. If he ever made it back, you could be sure I planned on telling him.

Krisz emerged from her side of the room, rubbing her eyes. "I think I'm going to try and get an early night in, too." She looked up at me, and gave a half-hearted smile. "He'll be OK."

By the next evening, Mitch had still not returned. We made up some excuse to keep the kids calm, but now both Krisz and I were becoming frantic. Damn him for doing this to us yet again. We didn't even know where to look for him, except to follow the well beaten path away from the shelter.

"They're all asleep," Krisz said as she joined me at the table.

I slid a cup of cider across the table to her. "Here, I found this in the stuff we took from the gift shop. It's not bad."

"Thanks." She took a sip, watching me from over the edge of her cup. After a moment she put the cup down and laid a hand on my arm. "You have to stop beating yourself up over this. He made his own decision, and you have a responsibility to the rest of the group."

I let out a sigh of frustration. "He had one too," I threw back at her.

"And he still does." She took another sip of her cider. "This is really good, thanks."

I jumped to my feet and began to pace. "He drives me mad." I spun to face her. "What exactly are we supposed to do now?"

She shrugged. "Nothing. Nothing but wait for him to come back."

Chapter Thirteen

By noon the following day we had run out of methods to soothe Jamie's growing anxiety. Krisztina had taken Ally and J.J. out for some air while I attempted to calm Jamie. I held his hands as I spoke in a soothing voice. "Just focus on me, OK? I need you to breathe with me." I bent down enough to catch his gaze. His tear-filled eyes darted back and forth, as though he was searching for his brother, somewhere beyond the shelter. "You have to be brave for Mitch, and trust that he'll come back."

"But he-" Jamie gasped, sending himself into a full blown coughing fit.

"Easy," I soothed him. "Breathe slowly." I drew in a sharp breath through clenched teeth. "Mitch has always come back, right?"

He nodded, tears flowing freely down his cheeks. His eyes were full of panic, making him look so helpless, which was exactly how I felt.

"He will come back this time too." I wiped his face with a damp cloth. "Keep breathing with me." I moved my hands to his shoulders and gently massaged his tight frame. "Come on, try to relax a bit." To my relief he leaned in to me. I reached for the salve I had prepared, careful to keep one reassuring hand on him. "I'm going to rub a bit of this on your back."

He nodded against my shoulder, still wheezing.

I kept rubbing his back until I felt the tension begin to leave his body. His breathing slowed, though his cough remained rough and obviously painful. "That's it, let yourself go." He shuddered as he managed a deeper breath. I shifted him around, letting his back rest against me. "Do you want me to hold you, or would you like to lie down?"

He shook his head no.

"Does that mean you want me to hold you?" I guessed.

He nodded, becoming heavier. I kissed the top of his head and snuggled him closer, careful to allow him room to breathe. His pants were getting too short, and boney wrists stuck out the ends of his sweatshirt. I'd rummage through the packed clothing for a few new pieces later.

The door pushed open, letting the afternoon light spill inside. Krisz poked her head in. I nodded for her to enter and Ally sauntered in. Krisz followed, holding a limp J.J. in her arms. I felt an eyebrow creep up my forehead and wondered how you could fall asleep in the snow.

Plopping down next to me and a sleeping Jamie, Krisz rubbed her tired eyes. She leaned in closer to peek at Jamie's face. "He's fine, now," I reassured her.

"What are we supposed to do now?" Obviously antsy, she jumped back to her feet and paced for a moment. "You want some of that cider?" Her head turned as she scanned the shelves.

I pointed to the jar in question, shifted Jamie and stood. Heading to the back of the shelter I settled him in his bed, careful to leave his head slightly elevated, and quickly checked his vitals. Satisfied, I returned to Krisz who was pouring hot water into two souvenir cups. I felt drained and discouraged. "I don't know what to do about our situation," I said honestly. I added some wood to the fire, not because it was cold in our shelter, but because I felt chilled to the bone.

"Here," she said, handing me a steaming cup. "What do you want us to do?" She stared at me point blank. "I'm not going after him, and I won't let you go either."

I knew she was right, in the sense that we couldn't risk having only one of us left to care for the kids. "We can't really pack everyone up and take them with us either." I was speaking more to myself than her.

She snorted, raising both eyebrows.

I tilted my head. "I wasn't suggesting it, just stating a fact." I sipped the warm liquid, tasting the tartness as I swallowed. "I don't want to have to leave him out there either…" I let my voice trail off.

We hashed out possibilities for a while, and must have fallen asleep because the cold from a badly closed door woke me. I looked over at Krisz who dozed peacefully beside me. Could

Mitch be home? I stood and nudged Krisztina from her sleep. I walked over to the door and tugged it open, taking a quick look outside. There was something lying on the path Mitch often took, so I ran out without my jacket to check it out. Ally's scarf lay in the middle of the path. My blood ran cold. She wouldn't have…

"Aleksei!" Krisztina's panicked voice called from the door.

I turned to face her, and my heart sank. I didn't need to hear it to know. Ally was gone. I hurried back to the shelter, wanting to make sure the boys were still there and I needed to see with my own eyes that Ally wasn't.

"Maybe she just went to the outhouse," I offered hopefully. But then, why would her scarf be on the path?

Grabbing hold of my shirt with both hands Krisztina was frantic. "We have to find her!"

Bile rose in my throat. "Dress the kids and I'll load the sled with emergency supplies." Unable to think straight, I pulled out our makeshift toboggan and threw on some extra blankets, a butane burner, cocoa, water bottles, and cups. Letting out a shaky breath I turned on the spot as I tried to clear my head. It looked more like I was packing for a picnic than a search and rescue excursion. To top it off, we wouldn't get far before nightfall.

J.J. was screaming at the top of his lungs, not happy about being woken up, while a disorientated Jamie was sitting up, rubbing his eyes. I grabbed Krisztina by the shoulders. "What are we doing?" I wasn't sure if we should go or not…nothing made sense.

She let out a breath in frustration. "You stay with the kids, I'll go look for them."

I took a step back, shocked by the proposition. "I can't let you go!" I passed a hand through my hair and tried to think. "You stay here with the kids, I'll go."

She shook her head. "No. If you didn't come back, I wouldn't be able to handle spring planting and all. The kids would have a better chance of survival with you."

That settled it. "Pack 'em up. We're all going."

She nodded this time, grabbed J.J.'s snowsuit and went to dress him. I looked over at Jamie. "You doing all right?"

He shrugged, and pulled on his own winter clothes without saying a word.

I grabbed a flashlight, some snacks and the hand warmers from the gift shop. This would have to do. In any case, I hadn't planned on being gone over night. "Almost ready?" I asked Krisztina.

"Yeah, just grabbing some extra diapers. Let's do it." She ushered Jamie along, holding J.J. football style under her arm. He had stopped crying and was wiggling his way out of her grip.

"I want to walk," Jamie said. He watched as I sat J.J. in a secure manner on the sled.

"Fair enough, but you can sit if you get tired." I braced myself against the shoulder straps and trudged toward the path Mitch used. I hope he and Ally would be found safe and sound.

"What's the matter?" I asked Jamie. We had been walking for an hour, and his pace had been slowing exponentially over the past ten minutes.

He tilted his head, struggling to catch his breath. "I'm OK," he insisted. He coughed a few times and turned to continue walking.

"Why don't you come sit with J.J. a bit? He might like the company," I suggested. Krisz helped Jamie settle behind J.J. and I drew in a deep breath before moving on. There had been no sign of Mitch or Ally. I was beginning to wonder if they had been abducted. Maybe the aliens had decided to move them out of their mining zone along with the rest of the townsfolk. If they were even still alive…

"Can we stop a bit?" Krisztina asked. "I think we could use a break."

I nodded, dropping the straps to the sled and stretching. The sky was indigo colored, and the snow covered trees seemed to glow in the light. I shot a weary glance down the path ahead, no wonder it took Mitch so long to come and go, the path seemed to go on forever. He certainly had packed this trail down.

"Here," Krisz said, offering me a pack of trail mix.

"Thanks." I turned to see the kids happily munching on their food. Rummaging around for the burner I set a pot of water on it to boil. Jamie was playing peek-a-boo with J.J., keeping him amused while they snacked happily on their granola bars and fruit snacks.

Kristina plopped down next to me onto the blanket in the snow. "I think we should head back," she said. "Who knows how much further until we find what Mitch had been talking about? We don't even know if they came this way." She wiped away a tear from her cheek. "I don't know what to do…"

"Then we should head back. Maybe Ally returned home while we were gone," I suggested.

Krisztina clamped a hand over her mouth. "Oh my God, I didn't even think of that! What if she came back and we weren't there?"

I rubbed a hand over my eyes, trying to wipe away the frustration. "Look, we're doing the best we can." I tossed a mound of snow down the path, my patience running thin. "I just can't believe she wandered off." I stood and brushed the snow from my pants. "Let's have something warm to drink and head home."

"Are you walking or riding?" I asked Jamie. J.J. had been secured in place, and our gear loaded up.

Jamie shrugged, without stating a preference.

Krisztina was anxious to get back to the shelter, in case Ally had returned, and was fidgeting. "Just get on and hold J.J., we're wasting time." She guided him rather firmly by the shoulders and sat him down before he could react. "Let's get a move on. It'll be dark soon." She stormed ahead of me.

I turned the sled around and headed after her. Jamie twisted around to see and toppled off the sled. "You're not going the right way, Aleksei," Jamie said in a panic. He stood and started off in the other direction. "Mitch!" he coughed a few times. "Mitch, where are you?"

I dropped the straps to the sled and ran back for him. Dropping to his level I held him firmly by the shoulders, keeping eye contact. "You have to calm down, now. I don't have what we need to deal with an attack." I gave him a moment to absorb that bit of information, and to calm down. "We're going back to the shelter, in case Ally and Mitch have come home. They'll be worried about us." I waited. Watching for a nod of compliance, then escorted him back to the toboggan.

Jamie climbed back on and pulled J.J. closer to him. "Do you think they'll be home?" he asked, his voice barely audible but hopeful none the less.

I sighed. "I want to believe it," I said honestly. I braced myself against the straps and began the trek home. Fortunately, Krisztina wasn't far ahead. It looked like her days of storming off were over.

We walked in silence for over an hour, keeping our glum thoughts to ourselves. Darkness had fallen, and without the sun's heat the cold seemed to pass right through our clothes. I could barely feel my hands or feet, but I couldn't afford to stop. I had bundled the boys up as much as I could and put pocket warmers between them and their blankets to keep them warm. Grateful that the moon crested over the mountain peaks, shedding enough light to guide our way without having to use our flashlight, I encouraged myself to move at a quicker pace than before. The thought of warming myself by the fire was almost as big a motivation as finding Ally home. My heart sank when I realized that we had never shown her how to maintain the fire. If she had made her way back, she was probably cold and worried. I gritted my teeth and forced myself to move even faster.

A few minutes later, focused on getting home, I slammed into an immobile Krisztina. "What'd you stop for?" I asked, my patience coming to an end.

She grabbed my arm. "I smell smoke. Mitch must be home, because Ally doesn't know how to make a fire." She tugged on my sleeve, urging me forward.

"I had a good rate going," I muttered as I dug in and started forward again. I couldn't deny the glimmer of hope I felt. The last part of our trajectory was covered on pure adrenaline.

As the door to the shelter came in sight we ditched the sled, each grabbed a child and raced for the warmth of our shelter. I reached the door first and flung it open a little too enthusiastically, but the sight that met me stopped me dead in my tracks. Krisztina slammed into me, startling J.J. "Now what?" she asked, exasperated.

My legs turned to lead and my stomach knotted, but I managed to move enough to the side to let her see for herself. I heard her gasp from behind as she caught sight of what had brought me to a screeching halt. Mitch and Ally were back alright, along with two of the blue-clad visitors. My mouth went so dry I couldn't speak, couldn't even make a sound.

Mitch came towards me and took Jamie from my arms. He glanced up at me quickly and whispered, "It's OK. Come warm yourself." He gave a half-hearted smile and closed the door behind me.

I felt the hair prickle at the back of my neck. Even if I had wanted to warm myself by the inviting fire, my legs were rooted firmly to the ground.

My heart beat wildly, and I could scarcely breathe. What was Mitch doing with them? I jumped back and slammed into the wall behind me, having instantly regained my mobility when one of the aliens approached. Losing my footing I fell back, shielding my head as the alien reached down for me. "No!" I yelled as I felt his touch on my arm. I didn't dare move, didn't dare look up.

"It's me, Mitch," a familiar voice stated calmly. "Let me give you a hand."

I blinked twice, trying to clear my vision. Though the aliens were still in the room, they now stood a fair distance from me. I wiped my moist, shaky palms on my pants and accepted Mitch's offered hand. "What's going on?" I whispered. The tremor in my voice was all too clear.

Chapter Fourteen

"Come on," Mitch urged me to join them at the table. "We need to talk."

"You think?" I stood now, uncertain of what to do. Krisz held tight to J.J., waiting for me to decide on a course of action. She appeared ready to bolt, and I understood the feeling.

"Trust me." His eyes pleaded with me.

I jammed a cold hand through my hair and let out the breath I had been holding. Feeling defeated, I closed my eyes in submission. "Fine, I'll trust you," I said through clenched teeth before looking up to hold his gaze.

Mitch nodded with a slight grunt. "Let's put the kids down first, so we can talk." He turned to step away from me.

I grabbed his arm and nodded discretely in the aliens' direction. "While they watch?" I was unable to hide the disdain in my voice.

He nodded, pressing his lips together. "Yeah…while they watch."

Krisz followed Mitch and laid J.J. down with the other two. I had yet to move from my spot. I stared openly at the aliens now. They were at least six feet tall, with a firm, almost identical, muscular build. They still had on their tight-fitting helmets with iridescent face shields so there was no way to see their features, not that I really wanted to, in case they were hideous. They hadn't moved, not even to follow Mitch and Krisz around the room with their gaze. My eyes narrowed. Maybe they were robots of sorts.

Mitch shot me an impatient glance from the other side of the half-wall, and moved toward the table. I waved him off, keeping my eyes on our two visitors, waiting for them to breathe. I let out a sigh. They were breathing, and not at the same time either…so much for the robot theory.

I moved to prepare something for us to drink, and because I needed to keep busy while Mitch, Krisz and our *guests* seated themselves around the table. My chest felt so tight and breathing wasn't getting any easier. With shaking hands, I took out cups for the three of us, not knowing if the aliens could or would drink. Turning to Mitch for help, I gestured my question discretely. He shook his head *no* when I held out the two extra cups.

Filling the mugs with boiling water, I could feel all eyes on me. Unable to control my nervousness, I spilled water over the edge of a cup and sighed. Oh, what I wouldn't give to be anywhere but here…

Krisz gave me a forced smile as I slid a steaming cup of cider in front of her. Mitch reached out for his and nodded for me to sit. "You are going to have to let them touch you," Mitch said in a controlled tone.

My head shot up. What, was he nuts?

Holding my gaze, he continued slowly, "It's their way of communicating. Amongst themselves they are telepathic." He cleared his throat and clasped his hands around his cup. "They won't hurt us."

I studied his features. Every fiber of my being was screaming for me to run as fast and as far away as I could, but something in Mitch's eyes held me. I shuddered. "What do we have to do?" I managed to croak out.

Satisfied, he held out a hand to Krisz and placed the other on the table near the alien. He nodded for Krisz to take my hand, but the alien stood and gestured with his black gloved hand for me to change seats. I swallowed hard and moved over to the right, sitting between the two aliens. I wiped my sweaty palms on my pants before placing my hands on the table.

Breathing through my mouth, I tried desperately to calm my inner shaking. A trickle of sweat ran down the side of my face. I flinched noticeably at the alien's touch, my trembling now outwardly apparent. I had to force myself to leave my hand under the alien's black glove and was immediately engulfed by a burst of light. I suddenly felt detached from my body as all the tension drained away.

Music filled the air, some kind of instrumental piece I remembered hearing once before. The tightness in my chest eased and I was aware of my body drawing in a deep, soothing breath. *Good*, a voice filled my head. *There is no need to fear us.*

"How can you say that?" I said. Whether it was out loud or in my mind, I couldn't tell. "I saw you attack people, saw you destroy buildings. We've seen what you are doing to our town." I remained surprisingly calm.

No one has been harmed.

"What are you talking about?" Mitch piped in. "If Jamie hadn't found Aleksei, he could have died."

"How can you be so sure others didn't die, crushed by falling buildings?" Krisz asked in an uncharacteristically composed tone.

No one has been harmed.

"What about all we've been through?" I asked. "We have suffered throughout this whole experience." I was angry, but I couldn't express it.

"Where are the others?" Krisz cut in. "What have you done with them?"

They had been placed in a remote area, but by now they have all rejoined other cities and towns. No one has been harmed.

"You destroyed our homes, our town, and that hurt us." Mitch came through with intensity.

I felt Krisztina's hope of finding her family flair up and filter across.

"What are you doing here with us? How long have you known we were out here?" I pushed ahead.

Since the beginning.

Mitch came through again, "We could have died, starved, hurt ourselves."

"You did hurt yourself," Krisztina added. An image of Mitch lying unconscious on the table flashed through my mind. "And then there was Aleksei, who ended up trapped in the snow."

We removed him from the snow.

I thought about that for a moment. "I would not have needed your help in the first place if you hadn't attacked the city." Images of my rescue faded in and out of my mind. I got the impression they were trying to keep me from seeing everything. "Why didn't you send us off with the others if you knew we were here?"

"Yeah," Mitch cut in. "Why did you leave us here to fend for ourselves?"

It was necessary. We needed to-

Mitch, Krisztina and I reacted at the same time, but something hushed us, numbed us and we became calm, almost mindless.

We must go, but we will return shortly.

* * *

I awoke with a kink in my neck and a stiff back. I grunted as I lifted my head off the table and tried to stretch. Mitch and Krisztina were still asleep, and still at the table with me. I felt a few of my vertebrae pop back into place, granting me some relief. Pushing away from the table, I stood and made my way to glance at Mitch's watch. 05:30. No wonder everyone was still asleep. I padded quietly over to the fireplace and threw in some birch wood, sending a curtain of sparks flying up the chimney. A wisp of smoke curled out of the hearth and filled the room with its particular aroma. I really liked the smell of a birch fire, I'd discovered. The flame had a blue hue to it when the paper-like bark was consumed, another reason why I liked this wood so much. Settling down before the fire on our homemade couch of camping mats on a rickety log frame, I drifted off to sleep again.

"You gonna sleep all day?" Mitch's voice, though it seemed far at first, became loud and clear as he shook me from my sleep. "Come on, the kids want your pancakes."

I rolled over and opened my eyes. "Why can't you make them?" I yawned and stretched. Passing a hand over my face, I tried to rub the fatigue from my eyes.

"'Cause yours are the best." Ally popped into my line of vision, wearing a huge smile and a mass of tangled curls.

I kept a stern look on my face as I drew in a long breath. "I am not too pleased with your little escapade yesterday. I'm not sure you deserve pancakes." I studied her face, watching her smile give way to a look of remorse. "On second thought, I think you deserve Mitch's pancakes for having pulled a stunt like that."

Jamie appeared by her side wearing nothing but a pair of too-short sweat pants. "No! He can't cook, and she was only trying to help find Mitch since you didn't want to leave us." He scrunched his brows into a serious expression.

Unable to contain myself, a laugh slipped from my lips. "I was just teasing about Mitch's pancakes." I sobered slightly and looked from Jamie to Ally. "But I need you to understand that you are never to try anything like that again, *ever*. Do I make myself clear?" I tightened my mouth a moment and focused on Jamie. "I know you let her out, because she can't reach the latch on the door. You have to trust our decisions and not try to take matters into your own hands."

They nodded without saying a word.

"Is that a promise?" I pressed on, needing them to understand the seriousness without trying to scare them into submission.

"Promise," they chimed back.

I nodded, satisfied. "Ally, get out the ingredients, and I'll be with you in a minute." I half expecting her to demand a *please*. Turning to Jamie I added, "You come with me. I think you could use some new clothes." I left Ally to get out the food while I headed back to rummage through our clothing reserves. It was a good thing we had grabbed a few extra pieces in various sizes. In all honesty, I never thought we'd still be out here after so many months. At one point, though, we would run out.

Jamie sat patiently as I checked the sizes. I handed him some jeans, a pair of navy sweats, three t-shirts and a hoodie. He looked at me shyly before leaning in closer. I couldn't help but note the pink tinge rising in his cheeks. "I need boxers too." His eyes darted back to the others.

I fished around another section of storage and pulled out a package of socks and boxers, mindful to place the socks over the boxers as I handed them to Jamie. I chuckled at the wave of relief crossing his expression. "Get dressed, and then come help with breakfast."

* * *

Huddled around the table as a family, I watched as Mitch poked at another bite of pancake. "Jamie's right. Your pancakes are better than mine."

Krisztina snorted. "Like we didn't know." She reached over and slid more pieces of cut-up food into J.J.'s bowl.

"I don't think I've ever tasted your pancakes," Mitch threw back.

She shrugged. "We didn't eat any of this stuff at home," she admitted. She reached for her cup and took a long drink, a faraway look on her face.

"Why not?" Jamie asked. "Is it because you don't like pancakes?" His eyes narrowed as he waited for her response.

Slowly, she shook her head and brought her gaze back to Jamie.

"No, I like pancakes. My parents were on all kinds of health-food kicks, like eating raw foods, sprouts and stuff you've probably never heard of."

Ally's nose wrinkled as her upper lip curled. "You ate raw meat? Eww."

Krisztina laughed. "No, we never ate meat. We ate our food raw and in its most natural state." She tilted her head slightly. "We had all kinds of sprouts that my parents grew on a regular basis, and we drank fresh juices and stuff." She shrugged with one shoulder. "It's actually pretty good, not to mention healthy."

Everyone had stopped eating and just sat there, almost open-mouthed. I'm not sure if it had to do with what Krisz was saying, or that she was actually sharing a bit about herself. "Do you miss it?" I asked. "The food," I specified.

She took another bite of pancake and chewed slowly, a smile spreading across her face. "Nope."

We looked at one another and started laughing. Mitch looked relieved. "Thank God, the last thing I'd want is for you to try some of those recipes on us."

That set us off on another round of uncontrolled laughing. It felt good to laugh. I gripped my sides and felt a tear trickle down my cheek as I let myself go. Mitch's look of horror at the prospect of eating sprouts was priceless.

"What about the stuff Aleksei made us eat?" Ally asked. "I don't know about you but I had never eaten that stuff before." Her eyes went wide as she emphasized her point.

Jamie crossed his arms and furrowed his brows. "I don't know, I thought it was pretty cool to eat like the Pilgrims and Indians used to."

Mitch leaned in close to me. "Is that what you told them?" he asked in a low voice.

I nodded. "I guess. I did what I had to; besides, it was sort of the truth."

Mitch raised his hands. "Not accusing anyone of anything. Like you said, we did what had to be done." He inhaled sharply. "I would like to discuss what we're going to do now, though," he said, his tone more serious now. "Don't think I'm OK with the situation anymore…knowing that we're under the microscope."

I pressed my lips together. "Tonight." I added another pancake to my plate, not meeting his gaze.

We kept busy throughout the day, focusing all our attention on the kids as we played outside with them, taking advantage of the warm sunlight. We let them soak in the hot spring for a while before bundling them up and rushing them fireside to dry off. Exhausted from all the fun and activity, they fell asleep as soon as their heads hit the pillows, which was good, since the three of us needed to discuss our options. We had barely looked at one another throughout the day, waiting for this precise moment when we would be able to talk freely and decide on a plan of action.

"I say we get out of here," Krisztina said, bringing her hands down on the table for emphasis.

Mitch rolled his eyes and waved an arm toward the door. "Lead the way!"

"Shh," I hushed him. "Keep your voice down. Ally must have overheard our conversation about finding you, which is why she took off. We don't need to worry them about this."

He shook his head. "They're out cold. No worries."

Krisztina clasped her hands together and leaned across the table, bringing herself closer to us. "I'm serious." She looked from Mitch to me. "When we were 'talking' with the aliens, I got a flashback from when I lost myself in the snow."

I nodded. I'd had that too. "Go on."

"That's why I didn't freeze to death. They'd found me." Her eyes held mine.

Mitch frowned. "How's that any help now?"

She waved him off. "They found me half-way through the barrier. It had me pinned down as I tried to get under it, but I was thinking that if we brace the snow and tunnel under it, we could get out and find our families."

We took a moment to let her theory soak in.

"How thick is it?" Mitch asked. "I mean, if we have to brace a twenty-foot long tunnel…"

Krisz chewed on her lower lip. "No, not twenty, but it's a bit longer than I am. If we wait for spring we could probably swim under it."

I nodded. "Makes sense. If the fish could swim through under water, we should be able to as well."

Mitch shook his head. "We couldn't get J.J. underwater that

long. Not without traumatizing the little guy."

"Caves?" I offered.

"Yes!" Krisztina jumped to her feet and headed for the bookshelf in the half wall. Dropping to her knees she searched the row of books and pulled one out with a smile. "Here," she said, plopping the book on the table.

I picked it up. *Montana Guide to Caving.* I glanced at Mitch. "She could be on to something, only I've never gone through caves before. Have either of you?"

Krisz shook her head, no. We both turned to face Mitch, who seemed to have turned a shade or two whiter. I studied his features, and watched as he struggled to conceal his unease. "OK, so caving is out." I wasn't going to press him.

"What? Why?" Krisztina jumped in.

I reached for her arm across the table. "Just drop it. We'll find another solution. Besides, the likelihood that the cave starts on one side of the barrier and ends on the other is pretty slim." I hoped.

She slumped back in her chair and crossed her arms. She shot a glance in Mitch's direction, catching on to the reason for my stand. "Oh," she said softly. "OK, we'll think of something else."

It took a moment, but then Mitch finally started to relax, or at least breathe. "Come on," I urged them to focus. "There has to be a way through." I turned to Mitch. "What can you tell us about their site?"

He straightened in his chair. "Their shelter is on the other side of the barrier, so there must be a way through."

"Unless they lower it to go through," Krisztina offered. "Which might be why some birds have been able to come back."

"Or they flew over it. We do get rain and snow, so it's not closed up." I leaned heavily on the table. "Could there be a door? Did either of you see them cross over?" They both shook their heads.

"They just showed up," Mitch said. "No noise or light, they were just there." He jumped back in his chair as his gaze shifted to something behind me, eyes wide. "Like that," he whispered.

The hairs on the back of my neck began to bristle. *They* were back.

Chapter Fifteen

Before any of us could react, the white light overtook us and soothing tones eased the tension while the aliens joined us at the table. We're going to have to teach them to knock, I thought to myself.

We said we would return.

"Yes," I agreed, "but you never said when." I was barely aware of the alien's touch on my hand.

That had yet to be determined.

"Why did you bother coming back this time?" Mitch piped in. "If you are not going to help us, what's the point."

I could feel Krisztina react in agreement, though she seemed far away and more subdued than the last time. It felt as though my mind was unable to think freely. Someone or something like a mental strait-jacket forced it to focus on the present conversation.

A slight burst of emotion came through from Mitch. "Why did you let us stay and struggle for so long? Why didn't you send us off with the others when you discovered us?"

A wave of some unknown emotion barreled through me, leaving a shiver to run down my back in its wake.

We decided to wait and observe.

"How long have you known about us?" I asked again, not having received a satisfactory answer during their last visit.

Since the beginning.

"That's what you said last time, be more specific," I demanded.

A pause followed, and I felt the vice-like hold on my mind tighten. *We watched the others free you from the rubble of the building. We watched as you took refuge below. From the beginning.*

Nausea overcame me and I felt the grip on my mind slip as the horror and repulsion at the notion flooded me. I wanted to strike out at them for having been so cold and heartless. We were nothing more than lab rats…

The light surrounding me faltered before regaining its intensity and I felt myself being pulled back to order. A buzzing between the two aliens erupted, blocking out any link to Mitch or Krisztina. I inhaled sharply and clenched my teeth as I waited for the unpleasant feeling to pass.

It was necessary. More information was required. We must go now, but we will return in three of your cycles.

Unlike the last time the aliens visited, we remained conscious after they left, though we never actually saw them leave. Mitch bolted for the door as soon as he could move, yanked it open and peered outside. He closed the door and turned slowly, shoulders drooping. Krisztina snickered. "Did you want to wave goodbye as they drove away in their spaceship or something?"

I shot her a glance but she only shrugged, turning to get something to eat. "What exactly is 'three cycles'?" I asked either of them.

"Days I guess," offered Krisztina. "Now we either have to take off before they return, or wait until they come back." She tossed packets of dried fruits and nuts on the table.

Mitch came back to the table, turned a chair around and straddled it. "We should wait. I don't think three days is enough to prepare for this kind of excursion, and they'd know we were gone almost as soon as we left." He tore open a package and emptied the contents into his mouth.

"It's not like they wouldn't notice either way," I added.

Krisz shook her head. "I don't think they're watching our every move." She went silent for a moment, chewing on her lower lip in thought.

I looked over at Mitch to see if he knew what she was referring to, but he just shrugged and took another pack of nuts.

She shifted in her seat and leaned in closer. "Look how long it took them before they showed up to get Aleksei out of the snow. I don't know how long I had been trapped either, but I do remember being half frozen. I kept having these weird dreams, so I must have been in and out of consciousness." She looked at Mitch. "Where exactly did you find me?"

Mitch picked a piece of nut from his teeth. "You were curled up in the snow against the barrier."

"No," she said. "You see, that's what I meant. That proves they pulled me out from under the barrier, since the last thing I remember was being wedged under it, unable to move." She shuddered at the memory. "I'd been there so long that I could no longer feel parts of my body. I was beyond cold."

"If we only have three days before they show up," I cut in, "then I agree with Mitch. I think we should wait until after their visit." I looked from Mitch to Krisz, chewing on the corner of my mouth. "This might be a long shot, but maybe we should watch our thoughts, in case they can read our minds when they're around."

Mitch leaned in closer and lowered his voice. "We should pretend we're planning a spring escape, when the weather's nice. That should throw them off and make it easier for us to keep our plans secret." He looked over my shoulder and I turned to follow his gaze, half-expecting someone to be there.

Krisztina tilted her head, shifting in her seat. "Do you really think it'll work?"

I shrugged. "We won't know unless we give it a try." I thought about it a bit, and how it felt when the aliens were close by. "It's not like we'd have to hold the thought, because we aren't able to focus on much when they're around. Maybe just keeping the thought of a spring breakout will be enough."

Mitch cleared his throat. "They freak me out. It feels as though they are controlling my mind when they're here." He shuddered slightly.

Krisz and I nodded in agreement. "I know what you mean," I added. A thought struck me. "We should add underwater to our breakout plan, because if they can read our minds we want to at least be on the same page."

"Makes sense," Krisz said. "Might seem too strange if we all have different scenarios, but 'swimming out' is clear enough." She stood and went to collect a pad and pencil. She quickly sketched a stream with a barrier over it. "Get a good look at this," she said pointing to the image. "In the spring, we make it to the barrier over a stream or river and swim out." She held the image in front of us, one at a time. Placing the image on the table she laced her fingers together and leaned in closer. "Now, what's the alternate plan?"

"I'm going to take off for the day tomorrow and check out the perimeter," Mitch announced. "I promise to be back for supper."

He added, looking at her with a scowl, challenging her to protest.

"You had better be," Krisz threw at him, not backing down.

"What do we tell Jamie?" I asked. "He's not going to like it." I could just imagine the panic after everything we'd just gone through. I was at a loss to come up with a story to tell him.

As if she was reading my thoughts Krisz voiced my concerns. "We can't tell him the truth, in case the aliens can read our minds."

Mitch ran his hand through his hair. "Tell him I went hunting."

"Gross," Krisztina moved to swat him on the arm but he caught her hand.

Raising an eyebrow as he studied her face, he added. "At least that would be an explanation he'd believe."

She pulled her hand from his and turned away as she stood, trying to hide the pink tinge blooming in her cheeks. "Whatever."

I shifted in my seat, lost in thought. We had to do something, and Mitch was the best one to check out the perimeter. Maybe there was a way through it. "OK, since we don't have much of a choice." I reached for the book on caving.

Mitch shot me a worried look. "What do you want with that."

I flipped to the back of the book where pull-out maps were attached. Carefully removing them, I handed one to Mitch, another to Krisz and I kept the third. "See if you can locate our area on the map, then maybe you could chart the location of the barrier."

We each spread out our thin paper maps across the table, looking for some clue as to where we were situated. "Here," Mitch pointed on his. "These are the cliffs we're in, beside the hot spring."

Krisz and I both stood to get a better look. She pointed to another location on the map. "Could just as well be here," she said.

I leaned in closer. "She has a point."

Mitch shook his head. "That's a mineral spring. Trust me. It's not the same thing."

"Oh," Krisztina said. "Yeah, they're not the same."

I looked from one to another, still not understanding how he could be so sure. Before I could ask about it Mitch pointed to another nearby location. "This is the gift shop we raided." He tilted his head. "I wonder if it's still standing. I think we would have noticed orange powder falling so close to us."

I shrugged. "What would it change?"

Mitch sighed. "Depending on where the barrier is we might be able to use it over night. You know, if it's on our way."

I felt my eyebrows come down in a frown. "Sure, makes sense."

He went back to studying his map, calculating the distance with his fingers. Without looking up he added, "Oh, and the difference between a hot spring and a mineral one is about the same as one of J.J.'s clean diapers versus a dirty one."

"People soak in something that smells like-" I started to ask but Krisz cut me off.

"-rotten eggs." She shot Mitch a glance, pressing her lips tightly together in disapproval. "Mineral springs kind of smell like rotten eggs."

Mitch snorted. "Call it what you like, they stink." He didn't look up from his map, but instead leaned in closer. He pointed to a spot on the map. "There's a small town over here. Maybe we could get news to them somehow."

Krisz leaned across the table. "No one lives out there anymore."

Mitch nodded as he stood. "You're wrong. It's a tiny excuse for a town with only a few hundred inhabitants, but it's a town." His eyes widened as he stared at us. "Don't you see? If we could let them know we're here, they might be able to get us out."

I felt hope surge inside my chest. Knowing someone might be there to help us, to get us home and out of our misery energized me. "Start by mapping the barrier, and then we'll check out that town." I folded up my map. "We should get some sleep." I looked over at Mitch. "I'm guessing you'll be out of here early enough."

He nodded as he finished folding his map and collected the others. "Yeah, but now I don't see how I can fall asleep."

Fifteen minutes later I eased my tired body into my sleeping bag, the glimmer of hope still there, even though we'd have to find a way to deal with the aliens. I smiled to myself as I heard Mitch softly snoring beside me. At least he'd be rested by the time he took off. Before I could tackle the alien problem I drifted off to sleep, unaware that it had happened.

Not surprised to find Mitch gone when I awoke; I started to prepare breakfast while the others continued to sleep. Lost in thought as I set the table, the grim reality was that regardless of which side of the barrier we were on, the aliens were still here. We never did find out what percentage of our planet was being destroyed. I turned at the sound of footsteps behind me. I could tell by the shuffle that it was Jamie. I drew in a deep breath and turned to face him. Smiling brightly I asked in a low voice so as not to wake the others, "Sleep well?"

He nodded, scrubbing his eyes as he stifled a yawn. He looked around quickly. "Did Mitch go to the bathroom?"

I shook my head slowly and cleared my throat. "Actually, no. He went hunting," I offered slowly, bracing myself for an outburst.

Jamie nodded. "Cool." Without the slightest protest, he headed off to get dressed so he could go outside and use the facilities.

I just stood there and watched, still expecting him to start howling any second, when the notion that his brother had run off again sank in.

I was wrong. Jamie headed outside and returned a short while later still in a good mood. Grateful, I felt a smile spread across my lips, then widen as I caught a glimpse of Krisztina as she made her way over, pushing a tangled mess of hair from her face. "What are you looking at?" She challenged.

I raised my hands as I bit back the smile, turned my back to her and pretended to focus on breakfast.

"What happened to your hair?" Ally asked with a hint of horror to her little voice.

That was enough for me. I burst out laughing and had to duck out of the way as she tossed the boot she had been trying to pull on. "I think she had a good night sleep is all," I offered.

Ally looked uncertain. "Then why is she still crabby?"

Krisz grunted in frustration, yanked on the door and stepped outside without buttoning her coat.

I dressed Ally for the cold and wondered if I should send her off behind Krisz or not. "You want me to go with you?"

She shook her head. "Nah, she doesn't scare me." She gave me a huge smile and stepped aside for me to open the door.

"Just give us a shout if you need help." I winked at her and watched as she ambled away from the shelter on the snowy path. I sighed. Spring would be so welcome.

"J.J.'s up," Jamie called from his place at the table.

I closed the door and turned to look over the half wall. J.J. was bouncing in his portable bed, drool running from the toothy grin. It wouldn't be long before he figured out how to crawl over the edge, I thought. He was getting so big. I made my way over, noticing the two tone color of his sleeper. He was soaked right through.

"I'll get some clothes out for him," Jamie said. He busied himself as I peeled the wet clothing from J.J.'s plump body.

"OK, little man," I said as I lifted him free of his wet bedding and pajamas. "Let's get you cleaned up." I set him down on a towel before the fire as I gave him a quick sponge bath.

"Here," Jamie said, holding out a diaper and a sippy cup.

I nodded, grateful for the help. It was kind of cool how everyone could step up and help out. With the diaper on I took the offered overalls and quickly dressed J.J.

Without having to ask him, Jamie finished setting the table just as the girls came back in. Krisz had managed to pull her hair into a pony tail, and Ally was sporting pig tails. Her hair had grown out from the short cut I had given her months ago. They were lost in an animated discussion, oblivious to us as they stripped off their winter coats.

Jamie just looked at me and shrugged, picked up J.J. and settled him in his highchair before sitting down at the table to wait. I took that as my cue to start on the pancakes.

No one mentioned Mitch's absence and there was none of the tension we had felt the last time he'd gone off. I wished he'd have thought of the hunting excuse before. The day passed quickly and without incident.

Before I realized it the time to prepare supper had arrived. Jamie and Ally hurried to the table when I started pulling out a pot to prepare the meal. Twisting his hands together Jamie fidgeted before me. I shook my head, anticipating his request. I raised an eyebrow slowly as I waited for him to come out and say it.

Ally let out a sigh and nudged him. "Want me to ask?"

He stomped his foot lightly. "Wait."

I turned to face him, giving him my full attention. "Yes, you can pick out something for supper."

His face lit up and without a word the two of them scurried off to raid what was left of our cans. We were starting to run low on supplies. Maybe it was time we got out of here.

The sound of an engine broke our usual silence. In unison, we all stiffened and braced for the worst. I looked at Krisz who was holding J.J. tightly, and mouthed 'stay here'. I grabbed my coat and went outside as she gathered the kids close and huddled down behind the wall.

My mind ran all sorts of scenarios, but seeing Mitch, grinning like a thief on the back of a snowmobile was not one of them. I hurried over to him as he pulled up to the door. Behind him was a sleigh filled with food and supplies. I looked over the sled in wonder.

Jumping down from the snowmobile he slapped me on the shoulder and nodded toward his bounty. "Help me unload this quick so I can hide the sled in the woods behind the outhouse." He started handing me bags of provisions. "We're going to enjoy the next few meals."

I grabbed a couple of the bags and turned back towards him, blocking the door. "I thought you were going to check out the barrier."

He nodded, shifting his armload of bags. "I was, but we talked about the gift shop last night and I decided to take a chance, hoping it was still standing. The snowmobile was a bonus." A smile radiated from his face. "And there are five more." He nodded for me to open the door, then added, "We're getting out of here."

Jamie and Ally hurried over to carry the bags back to the table, wasting no time to rummage through their contents. I shook my head and followed Mitch back out for another load.

Mitch handed me some bags before pausing. "I think I have a plan." His eyes searched mine as he obviously wrestled with his thoughts.

"I'm not the telepathic one, remember?" I teased.

He shook his head. "I was just considering what we'd discussed about being careful about our thoughts." He sighed, frowning slightly. "I want to try something next time they come back. Just trust me, OK?"

I shrugged. "Sure, but how can we help?"

He paused, twisting his mouth before he answered. "Just keep asking them questions, I'll let you know if it works." He held my gaze.

I didn't press him for information, not because I wasn't curious, but because I didn't want to give away his plan when *they* came back. I nodded. "Fair enough. Now let's finish unloading and hide this monster."

Chapter Sixteen

Two days later, we were ready for the return of our captors. We had deliberately talked non-stop about our spring, water-escape, hoping to overshadow any thoughts that might give our real plan away. Even if they scanned the younger members of our group, all they had heard was the fake plan. Another thing we had agreed upon was to try and emotionally overwhelm them, hoping to get a glimpse into their thoughts. It was just a theory, but having a plan made waiting a little easier.

Krisztina was fidgeting, pacing as she waited for them to show up. It had been a mixture of freezing rain and sleet all day, so no one had left the shelter. She pulled open the door again to peer outside. "Well, at least the rain seems to have let up. It's snowing now." She slammed the door shut with a grunt.

Mitch was sitting across from me at the table watching her. As for me, I tried hard to ignore them both while I read. I lifted my head to follow Krisz across the room to rearrange the shelves yet again. At least the place was clean. Clean, tidy, rearranged, reorganized...I shook my head and went back to my book. Out of the corner of my eye I saw Mitch drop his head and suppress a snicker. His head shot up and he stiffened. The uneasy feeling in the pit of my stomach let me know *they* were back.

The flash of light engulfed us and in an instant we were all seated around the table. Something seemed off, but not being able to think freely made it hard to follow up on my thoughts and impressions. There was an urgency, a tension surrounding us that had never been there before.

We do not have much time.

"Then why did you bother coming?" Krisz tossed back. She was obviously in a foul mood. "Why don't you leave us alone? Haven't you done enough, keeping us caged up here like a bunch of zoo animals?"

Mitch cut in. "Krisztina's right. We want to go back to our families. We don't want to be part of your boredom breaking entertainment anymore."

The light intensified, almost squeezing the air from my lungs.

Please, remain calm.

I forced a breath into my lungs. "When are you going to let us go?"

"I'm sick of living like a caged animal, like a caveman, for that matter!" The intensity in Krisz's thoughts increased and I caught a glimpse of our planet before my mind was redirected again.

"Stop that!" she yelled. "Do you have any idea how we feel?" Have you ever been held captive, away from friends and family?" She choked back a sob. "Do you even have family?"

I saw it this time, the images of their plans. Three other cities had undergone the same fate. Their long-term plan was to use the entire planet for fuel!

Mitch slammed his hand down on the table causing everyone to jump. "Why won't you let us go? What have you done with the others?"

The light and control they had over us faltered. I got a strange feeling that they really were trying to help but the images I had seen...

You must not call attention to yourselves. You must remain here until we tell you otherwise. You must trust us. The fate of your home rests on you. The intensity of the last sentence impacted with the force of a meteor.

I turned away from the table quickly and vomited all over myself. Krisz lay passed out on the table and I was vaguely aware of Mitch running for the door before darkness came crashing over me.

Mitch was shaking me awake, holding a hand over his mouth. "Come on, Aleksei, wake up. You really stink." He shook harder and I heard myself moan.

"Stop, I'm awake," I said hoarsely. The smell of the vomit overpowered my senses, and I gagged. I stood shakily and stripped out of my slimy clothes. I had no idea how long I'd been unconscious. Gathering them into a bundle I headed outside in my socks and underwear. "Bring me a towel, will ya?" I shot Mitch as

I closed the door behind me and hurried to the springs.

Dumping my soiled clothes near our wash buckets, I eased my body into the soothing warmth of the water. Tossing the rest of my clothing aside, I let myself sink below the surface for a moment. The image that flashed in my mind was so intense I gasped, taking in a mouthful of water. Struggling to sit up, I coughed out the water as my arms flailed wildly.

"Aleksei!" Mitch's strong arm pulled me upright as I continued to cough. He pulled me to the ledge where I vomited again.

I held up a shaky hand as he quickly passed a towel over my face. I sat back on the rocky ledge, submerged to my shoulders. The images were clear in my mind now, and my body shook violently as tears streamed down my face. "We've got to get out of here," I whispered.

Mitch, who was standing in the water fully dressed, sat down beside me. "What'd you see?" His voice was grim.

"They're not going to stop." I turned to face him. "They're like scavengers. They plan on using the entire planet as a fuel source."

His eyes held mine as he shook his head. "Then why bother helping us? Why take the time to remove the people before destroying the city? It doesn't make sense…" his voice trailed off.

I continued to shake uncontrollably as the images of their plan haunted me. I saw other places, other times, people piled into tiny parcels of land, too small to support life. No shelter, no food…people starving, dying in helplessness and fear. I could not remember ever feeling so small, so helpless in the face of impending danger. "We can't do this on our own. We have to warn someone."

We sat there in silence, Mitch still in his wet clothes, lost in thought. The sound of footsteps pulled me from my feelings of despair and I looked up to see Krisz standing over us. She looked from Mitch to me. Studying my face she said slowly, "You saw it too."

I closed my eyes and nodded. What could I say? The image had been more than enough.

Mitch shifted. "Then why didn't I see it?"

Krisz twisted her mouth, biting the corner of it. "Maybe you didn't really want to."

I waved her off. "Look, it doesn't change the fact that we have to get out of here and warn somebody. There has to be some way to stop them before it's too late." My voice dropped to barely a whisper. I couldn't imagine how we would manage against such a formidable opponent. I needed to think about this. Bracing myself against the rocky ledge behind me, I lifted my body from the water.

"Stop!" Krisz spun around, raised a hand to her eyes and held out a towel. "I'm going back inside."

My cheeks flushed as I realized what I had been about to do. I reached for the towel and stood, quickly draping myself with it. "Come on," I said to Mitch. "Get out of your clothes and let's head inside. We've got lots to think about." I held out a towel for him while he stripped out of his wet clothes.

We hurried back to the shelter, barefoot and barely covered, our bodies steaming from the hot spring. In all honesty, I was too numb to notice the cold. Fear gripped my heart and my thoughts raced as I tried to come up with a solution. Krisz heated up some broth for us while we dressed.

"Thanks," I said as I accepted the steaming cup. I looked at the table, covered in the books we had taken from the souvenir shop.

"So much for your cleaning," Mitch said as he sat down to sip from his cup. He leaned in closer, eyeing the sketches on the map of the area. "What are you doing?"

Krisz dropped into a chair beside him. She pointed to the pencil sketch on the map. "I was trying to figure out how far the barrier was from the center of town." She glanced up at us before continuing. "Then I used the distance to trace a circle around the entire city."

Mitch pulled the map in closer, examining it intently before pushing it away roughly. He leaned back in his chair and looked at me. "There's no way we could know where this thing is."

Slamming her palm down onto the table she stared him down. "Well at least I'm trying!"

I pulled the map back. "No, she might be on to something." I sat down to study it. I glanced over at Mitch. "You should take the skidoo and check it out tomorrow. Then we'll know for sure."

He leaned back in his chair with his arms crossed; a mixture of dark emotions overshadowed his face.

I held his stare. "It's a place to start."

He pushed back from the table and stood abruptly, knocking the chair over. He turned away and jammed his hands in his hair as he paced about. Spinning back to face Krisz he spoke through clenched teeth. "Don't you see?" He waved an arm outward. "We're all goners. There's nothing we can do that'll make a difference." The anguish in his eyes spread across his face.

I hoped he was wrong. I let out a long breath. "We might as well sleep on it. With luck, by tomorrow things will seem a little more encouraging."

Krisz just nodded before turning away. Mitch picked up his chair then took the map from the table. He went to sit by the fire without saying a word. I followed him with my eyes for a moment; then stood, pushed my chair back and paused, debating if I should study the map with him. I let out the breath I had been holding and headed for my bed instead. I eased into my blankets and stared at the low ceiling, my thoughts running rampant.

By morning I was exhausted and discouraged. I wasn't surprised to find Mitch's bed empty; I just hoped it was because he'd fallen asleep on the couch. I watched Jamie for a moment, sleeping peacefully and totally unaware of the darkness that shrouded his future. I sat up and rubbed my hand across my face before I eased out of bed to dress. The night had revealed little hope for our predicament. I let out a sigh of disgust. After having spent my life at my parent's side helping the less fortunate, there didn't seem to be anyone there for us now.

"Aleksei?" Krisz's voice was barely a whisper.

I moved away from our sleeping area to see Krisz standing by the door. I twisted my mouth shut to prevent any comments from slipping out this close to Jamie. I didn't need her to tell me Mitch was gone, and I wasn't surprised.

I tugged a sweatshirt over my head and quietly walked towards the door. Stepping outside and closing the door behind me so as not to wake the others, I raised an eyebrow and waited for the news.

"I'm going to go with Mitch to check out the barrier," she said matter-of-factly.

I studied her face, nodded curtly and turned back towards the door. "Be careful, and be home before dark," I called out over my shoulder before returning to the warmth of 'home'. What else could I say?

Time passed quickly once the kids woke up. Fed and dressed, I had Jamie and Ally practicing their reading and writing while J.J. piled up pots and containers on the floor near the fire. He seemed content to hide odds and ends in his pots before stacking more on top.

Jamie sighed, catching my attention. "It's your turn, Ally. Spell the word elephant," he whined.

I held up my hand to stop him. Something was off with Ally. She was almost always the ray of sunshine in our household, yet the light seemed to have gone out of her eyes. I reached across to her and gave her little hand a squeeze. "What's wrong?" I asked gently.

She lifted her eyes to mine. They glistened with the tears she'd been trying to hold back. "Nothing," she whispered before dropping her head.

I pressed my lips together, trying to think fast. Shooting a glance in Jamie's direction I caught his attention. "Why don't you and J.J. grab a snack?" I urged him on with a nod of my head and scooped Ally into my arms. Stepping around the boys I settled onto the couch with Ally nestled in my arms. I kissed the top of her head lightly and waited for her to say something. The subdued shaking of her shoulders told me she was crying. "Tell me what's wrong," I said softly.

Her little body shuddered against mine. "It's nothing," she whispered. Her voice muffled. "I think I'm tired from all the bad dreams last night."

She always sounded so old for her barely six years. I held her tighter. "Do you want to tell me about it?"

She shook her head and sniffed. "Are they gonna take us away too?"

I felt my body stiffen. In an attempt to conceal my reaction I shifted her in my arms. "No one will take you away. I'm here for you, we all are."

She nodded. I felt the hot tears as they soaked through my shirt. "Do you want to tell me about it?" I asked. Slowly, I felt her relax a little, but she remained silent. For a minute I thought she had fallen asleep, but then she peeked over my shoulder cautiously.

"I saw a whole bunch of people from our town, from when they were taken away. They looked scared and then I thought of my daddy. I really miss my daddy…" her voice trailed off.

"I know, honey, I know." I held on to her and rocked her slowly while my mind went rampant. We already knew that we had to get out of here, but if Ally was starting to get flashes as well, we'd better do it sooner, rather than later. I let out a breath. Hopefully, Mitch and Krisztina would find something quickly.

As if on cue, the sound of the snowmobile could be heard approaching. Jamie raced for the door and jerked it open. "They're back!" He yanked his coat from its peg, jammed his feet haphazardly into his boots and scurried outside, leaving J.J. at the table.

Ally was looking up, craning her neck to follow the activity. I stood and deposited her on a chair beside her brother. Laying a hand on her shoulder, I glanced quickly towards the door. "I'll be right back, okay? Stay with J.J. a moment." Not waiting for an answer, I followed Jamie out the door.

Jamie was sitting on the snowmobile, talking animatedly with Krisz as Mitch hurried to meet me. He clamped his hand on my shoulder as he paused to catch his breath. "Get the kids dressed, pack some food and we're out of here." He coughed a few times and gasped for a breath of air.

"Hey, stop a minute, will you?" I waited for him to stand and face me. I searched his eyes. "What's going on?"

He laughed as he leaned forward, still breathing heavily. "We found a spot to cross over, and it's only two miles from the edge of town." He seemed giddy.

"Do we have enough gas?" I couldn't wrap my mind around the actual possibility of being free. "How do you know that this other town is still intact?"

"No orange powder, and from our vantage point so high up, we could make out buildings." He stood tall and slapped me across the shoulders. "Well come on! We haven't got all day." He practically pushed me back inside.

As I stepped through the door I shifted into execution mode. "Ally, go pee then come back and dress J.J. We're going for a ride with Mitch and Krisztina before it gets dark." I took a backpack and filled it with nuts, granola bars, chocolate and other goodies. I added a change of clothing each and some water bottles. Slinging the pack over my shoulder, I scooped up J.J. and ushered Ally out the door with Jamie's winter clothes.

In record time, the kids were securely settled on the sled with blankets and the food pack. I nodded for Krisz to ride upfront and lowered myself onto the sled, nestling J.J. between my legs. Mitch finished refueling the snowmobile, tossed the empty fuel can toward the outhouse and straddled the machine. Shooting a glance at me over his shoulder, I gave him a 'thumbs up'. He nodded, turned away and started the machine. Startled by the loud roar, J.J. started to cry and almost threw himself overboard. I barely had time to grab hold of him as the sled lurched forward. He screamed frantically as I struggled to nestle him securely in my arms. Eventually, and out of sheer exhaustion, he finally fell asleep.

My back ached and my arms had cramped, but I held tight to the little man. I had no way of knowing how far we had yet to go, so I tried to focus on other things. Both Ally and Jamie watched as the landscape whizzed by, pointing to various objects here and there. I hadn't paid attention to anything but J.J. In any case, there wasn't much to see but trees and more trees. I assumed that we were lucky to still have enough snow to ride on but not so much that we sank into it. But then, I didn't have much experience with this sort of thing. I laughed bitterly to myself. I did have an impressive firsthand knowledge when it came to survival. The slowing of the snowmobile brought my attention back to the driver. Were we there, or had we simply run out of gas? We had not yet refueled and Mitch had strapped several cans to the back of the skidoo and sled. Not very cautious, I supposed, but considering the situation, it probably didn't matter.

Mitch got off and stretched before coming over to me. "This is as far as we go. We have to climb up that ridge." He pointed off to his left to an outcropping of rocks.

I stood J.J. on his feet and watched him waddle off a few steps before falling onto his knees beside Ally and Jamie. Unfolding myself, I tried to work out the kinks in my body as my gaze followed his outstretched arm. I let out a sigh. "You expect us to climb all the way up there?"

He laughed. "No, not there." He redirected my eyes and pointed again. "There, under the outcropping."

I shook my head. "I don't get it."

He shouted out to Krisz. "Keep an eye on the kids a minute, will you?"

"You should give them a snack," I offered. Turning back to Mitch, I saw that he had already started on ahead. Sliding, as I tried to catch up, I almost slammed into him when he stopped without warning. "Wow..." I had not realized how high up we were. The view was absolutely amazing. We stood a few hundred feet above a valley. The outline of a semi-frozen stream made its way through the sprinkling of trees below. I did a double-take. "Are those cows down there?"

The grin on Mitch's face was as good an answer as any. He clamped his hand on my shoulder and pointed. "Look there, through the trees."

I leaned in, squinting against the sunlight. "I don't see anything." But then it caught my eye...smoke. A thin wisp of smoke rose from a house almost hidden by the trees. My heart started to pound in my chest. "We're really getting out of here."

Mitch yanked me towards the kids. "Come on. Let's grab a snack and get on with it."

For a moment I remained with my feet firmly planted on the snowy ground. How could he think about food? Let's just get out of here!

Mitch tugged on me again. "Come on. It'll only take a minute, and we might need the extra energy."

I tore my gaze from the smoke and looked at him. Maybe he was right. "OK, but let's make it fast."

Not ten minutes later, Mitch and I were prying stones free, and digging through the snow. The way the stones lay askew at the base of the ledge created a perfect place to tunnel our way through under the barrier. Part of the outcropping supported the barrier and would protect us as we made our way out. It was almost like a mini-version of the ledge where we'd built our shelter. Maybe it was a sign...great, now I sounded like my mother.

"This one's stuck." I grunted as I tried to yank a rock from its nesting place. Bracing my foot against the stone wall, I pried it loose and tumbled backward onto Mitch's feet. He pulled me up from the shoulder of my clothing. "Thanks." I sat back a moment and caught my breath. I had removed my gloves to get a better grip on the rocks, but now my fingers were raw and numb. I shoved my hands under my arms to warm them a moment.

Mitch crouched down to check my progress. "Let me take over a bit." We didn't dare make the opening any wider than necessary, for fear the barrier would fill it in again. As it was, the barrier rested on the ledge above and then came down across the fallen stones. By carefully removing the stones that rested against the cliff, we just might have a way through.

While Mitch took over, I went back to Krisz and the kids for some water. "Everyone all right here?" Ally and Jamie were playing in the snow while Krisz carried J.J. around.

Krisz nodded towards our active little Eskimos. "They're fine. As long as they keep moving, but he's tired and if you two think it'll be much longer you might have to make a fire or something." Apparently going back was not an option.

I fished around the bottom of our pack for some hand warmers. Tearing them open, I shook them to activate the heat. "Put these in his coat pockets and wrap him up in a few extra blankets." I looked around, thinking. "Why don't you just pull him in the sled a bit?"

"Can we come too?" Ally and Jamie chimed in. I cringed as I looked apologetically at her. "Sorry. I'm going back to help Mitch." I grabbed two bottles of water and climbed back over to Mitch. Squatting down I looked into the tunnel we were creating. "How much further do you think we need to go?"

He sat back and took a bottle of water from me. He twisted off the cap, wiped his forehead with the back of his arm and downed half the bottle. "Two more feet I guess." He pointed to the tunnel. "Ease your way into it carefully. Tell me what you think."

I nodded, handed him my empty bottle and crouched down to peer inside. Crawling in on my elbows I made my way to the end. I figured we'd gone past the barrier's limit about three feet ago, but we couldn't just pop out anywhere...or could we? I crawled back out and went in feet first this time. I made myself as small as possible at the end and began removing stones, laying them at my head. Once I saw a glint of sunlight streaming through I tried to push the stones outward. A rush of tumbling stones caught my hand and forearm, causing me to cry out, startled. Gingerly, so as not to set more stones tumbling, I worked to free my hand. I could hear Mitch clearing the stones away from my head as I kept my focus on my task. Just as Mitch removed the last of the stones that separated us, I managed to free my hand. Pulling my arm free set a few more rocks tumbling, but opened the way to the other side. The last of the daylight streamed in, and it was the most beautiful sight ever.

Mitch literally crawled over me to get a look out. He swore under his breath, bringing my mounting elation crashing down. Now what?

Crawling back out so I could turn around I came face to face with Krisz and the kids. A look of relief crossed her face when she saw me. "Are you OK?"

I nodded, holding out my hand. "Nothing serious."

Her eyes widened. "But you're bleeding!"

Ally scurried away, only to return a few seconds later with the first aid kit. Her expression was serious as she took hold of my hand. "Maybe you should sit down."

Shooting an amused look at Krisz I caught her turning away to hide her grin from Ally. I was led by our littlest medic to the sled where she examined my hand more closely. Pulling a disinfectant pad from the kit, she struggled for a few moments, unable to open it.

"Here, let me." Krisz leaned in and opened it for her, withdrawing just as fast.

With a steady hand Ally cleaned the blood from my hand, exposing the scrapes and cuts.

"You see," I reassured her, "it's nothing serious." I held my hand out while she wrapped it in enough gauze to cover my entire arm. I heard a snicker from Krisz as she ushered two boys away, leaving Ally to tend to my hand.

Mitch stood over us and rolled his eyes as he looked at my hand. He urged me to follow him with his eyes. I couldn't help but wonder what we had to deal with this time.

"All done," Ally said with bubbling pride.

Standing, I reached down and gave her a quick hug. "Thanks." I bounded over to the entrance of our tunnel. We were running out of daylight and something had to be done soon. I followed Mitch inside, through our tunnel and out the other side. Great. We stood on a ledge overlooking the valley below. "How are we going to get the kids down from here?"

Mitch brought a fist to his forehead in frustration. "If we tie the kids into the sled, we could skid down the slope." He watched for my reaction.

I leaned over the 'slope' as he called it. It was so steep, I wasn't sure this was a good idea. I let out a breath. "We'd have to tie the sled to each of us and let it go on ahead of us."

He nodded. "We could go down on our backs with our heels dug into the snow." I wasn't sure it was the brightest thing to try, but then we were running out of time and light. We made our way back to the others where I opened the blankets in the bottom of the sled. "OK, guys, come here." I attached the backpack to the front of the sled, sat Jamie near the back with Ally between his legs and J.J. between hers. "I want you guys to lie back. I'm going to make papooses out of you." At least they thought it was funny. I folded the blanket over them, and wove the rope in a crisscross pattern over the top of them. I cut the rope we'd used to pull the sled behind the skidoo, and made three harnesses with it. "Let's get a move on!" I called to the others.

Together we hauled the sled to the tunnel, careful to keep the end with their heads up. It wouldn't do us much good if they panicked. One by one, we eased through. The sled only got stuck once, but angling it got it through. The last of the daylight slipped away as we crawled through. Mitch went first and he immediately tied the rope around his chest. Krisz and I were close behind.

Leaning over the ledge, Krisz shot a look in Mitch's direction. "You sure about this?" she asked in a tone barely above a whisper.

He handed her the rope and I fastened it securely around her, and then did the same with my end. "Let's get on with it." I said to no one. "Hang on there guys, this should be fun," I lied. Terrifying, yes, but fun, I wasn't so sure.

Together, we eased the sled over the ledge. The three of us sat on the edge and braced to support the weight. Leaning heavily on our backs, we held hands as we skidded slowly towards the valley below. The kids didn't say a word as the three of us grunted and endured the bumps and bruises our bodies collected. Snow had made its way into my suit and I hoped we'd reach the bottom soon.

The slope eased enough and we were able to stand. Shaking the snow and kinks out, I couldn't help the grin that formed on my face. We had made it. We were out, free and going to find our families. Throwing ourselves into a group hug we were ecstatic. At least this part of our nightmare was over.

The flash of light took us all by surprise.

They had stopped us. We barely had time to acknowledge the feeling of fear and doom before everything went black.

Chapter Seventeen

I awoke on the floor of an all-white, perfectly square room. There were no fixtures anywhere on the walls or ceiling; it was as though the room itself glowed and generated light. My clothing had been replaced with a form-fitting, seamless, white jumpsuit and my feet were bare. The warmth of the room couldn't stave off the chill that ran through me as I realized I was alone. I sprang to my feet and began to search for a door, for an opening, an intercom button, a window, something.

My heart pounded. I was trapped. Were the others alone as well? Jamie and Ally would be frantic, and J.J. would probably be howling at the top of his lungs. "Hey!" I shouted as I moved about feeling the walls. "Let me out!"

I went around the walls more times than I could count without any response. Without any sign from the others or even the aliens that had come to us in the past, my sense of despair grew steadily. I began to worry about my new family. Tears steamed silently down my cheeks as I slid to the floor in the corner of the room. My mind called out to the aliens that had come to us in the past.

The light touch on my shoulder made me jump as though something had exploded nearby. Two blue-clad aliens stood side by side. Were these the same ones? Why did they keep their helmets on? I sat there, unmoving, waiting for them to communicate, waiting for a sign. I stiffened as the alien laid his hand back on my shoulder. A burst of light filled the room and one simple command was given. *Follow.* There was nothing familiar about this touch, the light or the tone of the message. Feeling even more isolated than before, I stood and followed the aliens out of the room.

The narrow corridor was just as bereft of style and items as the room had been. As I moved ahead, sandwiched between the two guards, or whatever they were, I noticed that I could see into other rooms as I passed by. I stopped dead in my tracks as I caught a glimpse of Jamie's tear streaked face. He was obviously gasping for air. I began tapping on the window, frantically. "Jamie! Jamie, I'm here!" I turned to the guard behind me and grabbed hold of his shoulders. "Let me in there! Can't you see he needs help?" They grabbed my arms and started to half-drag, half-carry me down the hall. "No! I have to go to him!" I twisted and squirmed, pushing against them as I kicked wildly about. "Let me go!" I pleaded as they carried me away from Jamie. "You're gonna kill him! Stop!"

My world went silent as darkness engulfed me.

Opening my eyes, I once again found myself on the floor, in the middle of a barren, white room. Only this time, there were eight beings surrounding me. The image of Jamie came rushing back. "Where's Jamie? Let me go to him, he needs help." I tried to keep calm but there was no way to control my shaking. The beings just stood there in a semi-circle before me, not even moving. "Let me go to Jamie, please." They didn't even flinch. I made a move to leave the room, but there was no door. I moved around the perimeter of the room as I had done before, this time I kept an image of a door, of the hallway in mind. My hand passed through the wall. I looked back to see if any of the beings had made a move to follow me and slipped silently into the corridor. I could hear my heart pounding in my ears, my breathing labored. Jamie, focus on Jamie. I moved along the narrow passage, paying attention to the walls, hoping to get a glimpse of the others. Ally was on my left, curled up in a ball in the far corner of the room. Door, focus on the door I told myself.

Ally looked up from her corner and flung herself into my arms before I had even crossed into the room. Maybe it was better that way. "Shh," I hushed her. "Don't make noise." I moved slowly down the corridor, keeping an eye out for the others. Ally had a death grip around my neck, but she kept quiet.

This was the strangest place ever. White, and more white. No contrast, no decorations, nothing. The corridors were high and narrow, and the floor was almost soft to walk on.

I stepped back a bit as something on my right caught my eye. Krisz was moving about the room in total frenzy. I focused and slipped into the room. She froze in place, not sure what to do. I placed a finger on my lips to silence her and took her by the hand.

Stepping back into the hallway, I continued my search for Jamie.

J.J.'s cell was next. Holding hands, we slipped into the room. The little man was asleep; his cheeks were tear stained and his skin red and blotchy from crying. His nose had been running and he must have smeared it across his cheeks. Krisz reached down and gently scooped him into her arms. A shudder and a muffled sob racked his little body. If they let a baby cry himself to exhaustion, I could only imagine how we'd find Jamie.

We walked double the distance we had just covered before finding Mitch, yet there was still no sign of Jamie. God, please keep him safe, I prayed. Krisz and I held one another by the forearms and crossed into Mitch's room. He whirled around, eyes darting to and fro like a wild animal. I raised a hand to stop him and urged him forward. He and Krisz grabbed my arm as we once again slipped into the corridor. If only we could find Jamie. Then what? We didn't know where we were or if there was even a way out.

We kept on walking, unaware if we were simply turning in circles. What if he was lying under the window? We might have passed him by. Do we go back or do we continue? I couldn't even risk discussing it with the others. With every step I feared coming across one of the beings. I couldn't let them stop me from helping Jamie. I thought it odd that there were no guards, but then there weren't really any doors in the rooms either.

Mitch pulled back and pointed to the room I had just passed. A foot, barely visible from the window, moved. I hoped to God it was Jamie. Who knew how many others might be stuck up here?

Locking arms, we moved through the wall and I handed Ally over to Mitch. My chest tightened, it was Jamie. Mitch stood back and let me check out Jamie, who lay in a crumpled heap on the floor. His lips were blue and his breathing raspy, labored and very shallow. His pulse raced. "We're here, Jamie. Try and relax, we're here," I repeated to him softly. His eyelids fluttered but did not open. I sat behind him, holding him in a semi-sitting position and continued to talk softly to him as I massaged his neck and shoulders.

Mitch looked at me, not daring to speak. Tears welled in his eyes. I couldn't help but think we should have left well enough alone, that we should all be in our shelter, safe. Not wearing white stretchy suits, in white rooms, away from anyone or anything familiar.

Mitch and Krisz sat down, one on either side of me, each still cradling a child. We leaned on one another and cried together. It took a while, but Jamie's breathing slowed, and his body started to relax. My arms and shoulders burned and I needed to move, but I remained huddled with my group, my family.

I guess I must have fallen asleep, because when I looked up, the familiar forms of our visitors stood at our feet. One member of the group raised a hand telling me to stay put. Looking down at Jamie I saw that his color was back to normal and he now slept soundly in my arms.

Reaching out to touch me, I tried to hold steady when he laid his hand on my head. The familiar light and feeling surrounded me, relieving some of the tension I'd been carrying. I actually felt some comfort in his presence.

We will bring you back to your shelter. You can tend to your needs there.

Images of food and clothing came to mind.

You will have one cycle before you return to meet with our…

My mind was bombarded with images of a parent, king, government head, manager, military commander. "Leader," I offered.

There does not seem to be an equivalent, but Leader will do. You will understand more after the meeting.

And just like that we were home again, the lot of us piled onto the couch before a welcoming fire. I stood, lifted Jamie into my arms and brought him around to his bed. None of the others were awake. I peeled off the white jumpsuit and put him in a pair of sweats and a t-shirt. I did the same thing with J.J. and Ally before shaking Krisz and sending her off to bed. I tossed the jumpsuits into the fire, feeling the overwhelming urge to burn them. I pulled a t-shirt over my head, threw on a pair of sweats and wool socks and padded to the single butane burner to heat up some water for tea. I tossed some clothes onto the couch beside Mitch, but he remained oblivious to his change in surroundings.

My eyelids drooped as I stared into my now cold cup of tea. How many nights had I spent like this with my parents as they discussed the despair of the situation? They were faced with hopeless situations on a daily basis, yet they honestly believed that they somehow made a difference. How did that country singer put it? Something about trying to put out a fire with the moisture of a kiss…a feeling I could relate to.

I looked up, surprised to see Mitch coming in from outside. I hadn't even noticed he'd stepped out. "Why don't you go to bed?" he asked. "You were drooling on the table not five minutes ago." He yawned and stretched off to the side. "Come on. We could use a few good hours sleep."

I offered him a crooked smile and a nod. "Sure. I am beyond exhausted." The words sounded slurred. It wasn't as though we could do anything about our situation. I moved to my side of the room and eased myself between the layers of my blankets. It felt like pure bliss. I must have fallen asleep before my head touched the pillow, and I'd always thought it was just an expression.

The smells of cooking seeped into my sleep. Inhaling deeply I turned in my bed, pulling the covers tightly around me. My mouth watered, teased by the enticing aroma of bacon and eggs. Oh, this was one dream I did not want to wake from.

Something nudged my foot but I waved them off. Please don't take me from my sleep just yet. The smells grew stronger. Mitch's voice finally registered. He was talking to me. I sat bolt upright and scrubbed my eyes. Someone *was* cooking bacon. "'Come on," Mitch said in a flat tone. "We don't have much time."

I passed a hand through my hair and climbed to my feet. "Oh." I looked at Mitch, then over to the table. *They* were back. "Give me a minute, OK?" I watched as he went back to the table; then I stripped off my sweats and pulled on a pair of work pants and changed my socks. I scooted around from the half-wall and pulled on my boots before heading outside. My heart felt heavy. "Mom," I whispered as I walked. "I really wish you were here. I can't do this anymore." I took a few minutes to compose myself as I sat there on our compost toilet. Then it hit me, just how ridiculous it was to have made a compost toilet when these *guys* planned on destroying our entire planet. I laughed. I laughed until I cried.

"You Ok in there, Aleksei?" Mitch's voice called out.

Pulling myself together I stepped out of my temporary sanctuary and faced Mitch. I scanned his face. Was he still just fifteen? Or was it sixteen by now? He looked like a man, a father, caregiver and provider. When I met him, he was a boy, a brother, a student and a jock. His eyes held mine and I took a deep breath before giving him an excuse of a smile. "I'm OK."

He followed me back to our shelter where the others were waiting to eat. Oh, yeah. We always waited for everyone to be seated to eat. I felt so detached from everything, it was scary. Something was off but I couldn't seem to put my finger on it. "Are *they* actually going to eat with us?" I asked Mitch under my breath.

He nodded then shrugged. "They did bring the bacon and eggs."

My face twisted into a look of puzzlement as I stole a glance in their direction. They were seated at each end of the table, but stood as we made our way over. They indicated that they wanted each of us to sit off to their right. I had J.J. and Krisz to my right, leaving Ally and Jamie on Mitch's side. As soon as we were seated I watched as the aliens brought their hands to their helmets and unsealed them. I turned away, not wanting to see what was under there, and the gasp from Krisz supported my decision.

After a moment of silence I opened my eyes. My breath caught in my throat as I got a good look at our captors. I was dumbfounded, my gaze riveted to them as I examined them unscrupulously. They were beautiful. Chiseled works of art to be presented in a museum, with their midnight eyes, dark lashes and copper skin, topped off with wavy locks of ebony hair.

Even the kids stared openly. Mitch cleared his throat. "Maybe we should eat before it gets cold."

Jamie held out his hands. "I'll say grace."

I was surprised when 'Zeus' and 'Apollo' accepted to join our circle as Jamie offered thanks, but then, they had seen our thoughts and memories. Mitch elbowed me, bringing me out of my daze. He pointed to my plate. "Eat. They were nice enough to bring breakfast."

I frowned. Did they go shopping before they came here? I picked up a piece of bacon with my fingers and took a bite. Oh, this was really good. Mitch was attacking his plate while Krisz was slowly maneuvering her fork towards her mouth, mesmerized by our guests.

"You should have taken off your helmets before," Ally said, making the comment we had more than likely all been thinking.

I watched them from over my plate, unable to neglect my food any longer. I dropped my fork when the one to my left, Zeus, spoke. "We must keep it on when we are on duty."

"Hey," Jamie interjected. "You can speak!"

Apollo nodded. "Without the helmet, yes." He paused to take another bite of his food, chewing slowly, as though he was savoring every bit of it.

"That's silly," Ally added. She put her fork down and stared at Zeus, point blank. "You should have taken them off before. You scared us, and that's not very nice."

Out of the mouth of babes, I thought.

"You have given us much to reflect upon," Zeus said in his smooth, baritone voice. He put down his fork and pushed his plate away. "We do not have much time before you are to be..." his voice trailed off.

An uneasy feeling settled in the pit of my stomach. To be what, I wondered. Interrogated? Relocated? Eliminated?

Zeus caught my gaze and held it. *None of those, so please, trust us.*

I honestly didn't know how to react to that. Trust them, after the destruction of our city, and God know how many others? Hey, wait a minute, you can read my mind without touching me? I thought.

Touching provides us with total truth.

I nodded. I couldn't help but wonder how they planned on carrying out this meeting. I didn't think the kids needed to be traumatized again.

We can take you one at a time.

My stomach lurched. Not the kids, they cannot go alone. One of us has to be with them at all times.

We understand. We will try to respect your wishes. Are you ready to come with us now?

I felt my insides begin to shake. I knew there was no getting out of this, so I might as well get it over with. I had every intention to be there holding the kids for whatever they had in mind. I didn't even have time to finish my thoughts before I realized that I was lying on a raised platform, surrounded by nine helmet-wearing, blue-clad beings. I was relieved that no one was touching me yet. A small burst of light/thoughts let me know that at least one of our two Greek Gods was in the room with me. I tried to turn my head to the side, but realized that I was being held firmly in place. My heart rate kicked up and I began to feel very uncomfortable. I felt a hand on my right shoulder, Apollo. A wave of reassurance was pushed through me and I felt my body relax a little. A fraction of a second before the others laid their hands on me, Apollo told me to remain calm, that he'd stay with me through it all.

I gasped as a feeling of panic exploded when the others touched me. Apollo immediately intervened, causing the feeling to diminish somewhat. It felt as though my body had been compressed, but slowly, the feeling dissipated and I drew in a deep, shaky breath.

Explain.

Explain what?

Your kind seem almost paradoxical. You have strip-mined, razed entire forests, fished entire species from bodies of water, polluted and destroyed your own habitat. You need something and take it regardless of the effect on your own kind. Animals are disappearing at an alarming rate. We have observed weapons testing, war and entire populations dying of starvation. You seem to have a blatant disregard for your world and your kind.

I did not disagree with them. I could not. Lord knows, I had seen a lot of this first hand with my parents.

And then we find you.

I don't understand.

You are the youth of your species, are we correct?

Yes.

You are a stranger to the other members of the group.

Well, I was, but what does that have to do with anything? A strange buzz of activity circulated as if they were discussing something just out of earshot. I wondered what Mitch and the others were doing, if they were all right, if they were worried about me.

Why did you bother with the others?

I don't understand your question.

We have watched you from the beginning. All the trouble you gave yourselves to create a dwelling, to produce food, to care for one another. Images of all the work we'd done flashed in my mind. Seeing us struggle as we tilled the soil and stored food for the winter brought back memories. The image of Mitch hurt after having falling in the woods, and Krisz, half frozen passed by. My gut tightened as I saw Jamie gasping for air, isolated in his cell.

"Stop!" The emotions felt as real as when these events had happened. I drew in a sharp breath as my body began to shake again. Will this nightmare ever end?

That same forced calm I had felt before came over me. I became disorientated, as though they were picking my mind apart. I hoped they wouldn't do this to the others.

Their wellbeing is truly important to you.

Yes.

I was drained, physically and mentally by now.

In your mind there are images of you and your parents helping others. Are there more like you?

More like me...you mean helping others? There are people fighting to stop pollution, to save our forests, to prevent children from dying of starvation and illness. Yes, there are many more.

In a flash, the room was empty except for Apollo. He had removed his hand from my shoulder, but kept contact with me just the same. *They need to discuss a few things, and they will also confer with the other two caregivers of your group.*

"They don't need to talk with little ones?" A wave a relief crashed over me.

They may not have to. I will accompany you back. Zeus, as you call him will go with the other. Mitch.

"Don't you have names?" I probably should mind my own business.

None are needed. We all have a distinct energy signature. You yourself recognized mine from the others, he paused. *We should go.*

"Aleksei!" Ally rushed into my arms. "Are you OK?"

I gave her a great big hug. "I'm fine." My heart swelled with the love I felt for each member of our group. I planted a kiss on top of her head. "Where are the others?"

She covered her mouth with her hand and giggled. "Outside, Jamie was too scared to go to the bathroom by himself, and J.J. was sleeping in Krisztina's arms. I told her I would watch him but she didn't want to put him down." She shrugged. "I'm not scared."

I hugged her. "Not scared, eh? How about hungry?" She kissed my cheek and pushed away from me. I set her back down and she scurried off to our special snack basket. I turned back to see Apollo watching. He had taken his helmet off and I couldn't help but be amazed by his beauty. And yet, such beautiful people were doing such horrible things.

The door opened and Jamie scurried in with Krisz on his heels. She had draped a blanket over the sleeping toddler, still cradled in her arms. Relief washed over her face. "You OK?"

I nodded. "Did you go yet?" I asked, but I could tell by the tightness around her mouth and the worry behind her eyes that she had not yet had her turn. I gave her a slight smile of reassurance. "It's not that bad."

She nodded; then settled herself on the couch with J.J. who slept soundly in her arms. She rocked him quietly, staring off into space.

"How long ago did Mitch leave?" I asked her, causing her to jump. "Sorry."

She forced a smile. "He left about an hour after you."

I had left from the breakfast table. "An hour? Are you sure?" How could it have been so long? It felt as though I'd only been there for about an hour. "And how long ago was that?"

She shrugged. "Mitch had the watch, and Jamie kept asking him over and over how long you'd been gone."

Jamie appeared from around the wall. He held out Mitch's watch. "He said I could hold it until he came back. I think he just wanted me to stop asking."

I took the watch and examined the screen. The chronometer was running. "Did Mitch set this when I left?"

Jamie nodded. "Uh, huh. He didn't have time to change it before he left, so it still shows your time."

I handed him back the watch. "Take good care of it." I had been gone a little over six hours. I could not believe it. Maybe that explained why I'd felt so drained after they had scanned my mind. I shuddered.

"You OK?" Ally asked as she climbed up on my lap.

I forced a smile. My stomach grumbled and she giggled. I guess that explained why I was so hungry as well. "How about we prepare something for supper? Mitch will be starving when he gets back."

She shook her head.

I frowned. "No? What do you mean, no?"

She smiled a Cheshire Cat smile and covered her mouth with her hands.

"I suppose you know something I don't?" I raised an eyebrow as I examined her features.

"I know too!" Jamie popped up beside us.

"Shh!" Ally scolded him. "It's a surprise."

"Well I'm hungry now. Could I at least have a snack?" I asked, watching her exchange glances with Jamie. The little bug was actually debating on whether I could have a snack or not. I laughed. "Just a little one, please?"

She twisted her mouth and her grey-blue eyes twinkled with mischief. "Well OK, if you really can't wait for the surprise."

Mitch chose that moment to reappear. I stood and escorted him over to the couch. He was pale and shook slightly as he let me guide him. "You OK?" I asked, loud enough for his ears only.

He nodded, closing his eyes as he sat. Krisz clutched J.J. tighter in her arms and had begun to visibly pale. I gave her arm a squeeze as I turned to face our guests. I stiffened when I saw that six of them stood by the door. No wonder Krisz had frozen.

Each of them removed their helmet and placed it against the entrance wall. Zeus stepped forward and gestured to the group of Greek Gods standing behind him. "May we join you to continue our discussion?"

Ok, not what I had expected. I nodded. "Sure, we can just turn our couch around so we can all see one another."

Zeus shook his head. Allow us. A flash of light filled the room and a single large table with sufficient seating replaced our furniture. A platter of cheese burgers, salad and fries filled the center of the table. I looked over at Mitch who was standing next to Krisz. "Did you order out or something?"

He shrugged. "They asked." Ignoring me, he took a place at the table. Everyone followed suit, leaving me to watch. Mitch lifted his eyes to mine. "Well, come on." A tired grin spread across his face. "You don't want to miss out on this."

I sat between Ally and Apollo, eyeing the food. The smell was enticing and my mouth started to salivate. "You could have made a healthier choice," I said without much conviction.

Mitch snorted as he passed the food around. "You made us eat *healthy* enough to last a lifetime."

Everyone laughed as they passed the food around. "Wait," Jamie cut in. He took the hands of those on each side and the rest of the table followed suit. "Thank you, Lord, for our new friends, for keeping us all safe and for this wonderful food. Amen." He reached out and hurriedly took a huge bite of his burger.

I burst out laughing and winked at him from across the table. "That has to be your fastest, yet most sincere thanks yet." Picking up my burger I took a bite and let the flavors fill my senses. Oh, it was hot, juicy and very, very tasty. For the next ten minutes not a word was spoken. A few smiles were exchanged, but this was a communion of our stomachs. Now I understood how food could bring comfort.

"Are we going to be able to go home now?" Ally spoke, putting a brief stop on the chewing.

Everyone turned to Zeus, but the one to Ally's left answered. His hair was a little lighter, but they all seemed to share the dark eyes and copper skin. "You can call me Thor," he nodded curtly.

I frowned. I know I had referred to them as Greek Gods, but wasn't Thor Norse or something?

He smiled, his charismatic features radiating gentleness. Funny he should choose the name Thor, I thought. He caught my stare and nodded briefly. "I preferred the sound of that name, and you had a wealth of information." He glanced around the table, bringing his eyes to rest on Ally. "Let us finish our meal, and then we can discuss what happens next."

She shrugged one shoulder before stuffing more fries into her mouth, apparently satisfied with the answer. I couldn't help but feel uneasy. Until I knew what the situation was, I couldn't imagine it getting much better.

Chapter Eighteen

The instant we had finished eating everything vanished from the table. One of the aliens tended to the kids while we began our discussion. I tried to keep my breathing under control and the unease in the pit of my stomach at bay.

Thor spoke, "Please, do not ruin your meal with such anxiety. It has taken us a long time to observe the situation before coming to this decision." He looked at the three of us. "I want you to know that there is a…" The corner of his mouth curled into an amused smile. "…Greek God in each and every one of your government offices as I speak with you." He looked from Mitch, to Krisz, to me. "What will be said here will be transmitted to each of them, so they know just how close they came to premature destruction."

I shot a glance in Mitch's direction. My heart rate started to go from a walk to a sprint. The words 'premature destruction' were not to be taken lightly. I forced my attention back to Thor and blushed when I saw that he was watching me. I nodded for him to continue.

He drew in a breath. "We had been observing you, your world, for some time. We do not take what we do lightly. Just as you need a fuel source to survive, so do we. From our observations, we have seen you cause more destruction over the past 50 years, than has yet to be observed on any other planet. You are ravaging the planet, destroying ecosystems, eradicating animals and people at the speed of light. From where we sit, you seem to show no remorse. You want, you take…so, we did the same." He paused and let the words sink in.

I cleared my throat. I was still unsure where this discussion was leading. "But some of us do care." My voice sounded meek compared to his.

"Yes!" his enthusiasm caused the three of us to jump. "Don't you see? Having been given the chance to observe you has made us aware that our judgment was wrong."

"Us," I repeated in disbelief. "Six kids amidst an entire planet of people."

He nodded. "When we saw the younger one so insistent that you were trapped and in need of assistance, it caught our attention."

Mitch spoke up. "I don't understand. How did that even matter to you?"

Thor smiled at Mitch like a grandfather would to a child. "Children mimic their elders. Had your people truly been self-serving, you would not have stopped. You would have saved yourselves." He shifted his gaze over to Krisztina. "They stopped for you, and although you were far from appreciative, they took you with them. When you refused to cooperate with the shelter or the crops, they were patient." He studied her face, now enflamed with shame.

"I helped with other things," she said in a barely audible tone.

"I am not saying you did not contribute," Thor continued. "I am saying that you should have given up, you should have starved, or died of exposure." He looked directly at me. "You built an evacuation chamber that does not harm the environment, but under these circumstances, why bother?" He held my gaze, waiting for an answer.

My mouth was dry. "It was the right thing to do…" My voice trailed off.

He smiled openly now. "Yes," he said softly, "and had you been the children of self-serving humans, the result would have been different." He watched us, waiting.

Krisz shifted in her chair. "He grew up in a life of service," she offered.

"I am aware of each of your backgrounds," Thor confirmed. "However, in this situation, it was a choice. His knowledge was beneficial to the group, I agree, but you could have eaten the food removed from the fallen buildings." He sat back and drew in a long breath. "You became a micro community. You taught the children, learned new skills, worked as a team."

I raised my eyes to meet his dark ones. "What is going to happen to us now?"

Apollo cleared his throat. "We are going to stop harvesting your planet. We will give you the chance to change your ways, but if we see you continue on this path of mass destruction, then there will be no reason why we should not harvest it for our own use."

A chill ran up my spine. Was this a good thing? Would it even make a difference?

Ally came around my chair and climbed onto my lap. I gave her a kiss on the head and leaned in closer to say something to her. "Why don't you go back and play with the others."

She shook her head. "No, let me talk." She looked at Thor and held his gaze. "Why don't you help us?"

That caught him by surprise. The strange buzzing was back, they were probably communicating again.

The three of us just stared at Ally. I leaned in closer. "How did you know what we were talking about?"

She tilted her head to look up at me. "I saw the pictures in my head."

I clenched my teeth together. Why would they show this to a child?

"Why, you ask?" Thor questioned me. "You yourself as a child had been in the middle of man at his worst, and yet you try and protect these children from the truth."

"Pain and suffering are not the norm. Children shouldn't be subjected to it," I replied.

He smiled that slow, patient smile again. "Unfortunately, on your planet, pain and suffering are the norm. Even amongst families there are parents responsible for the death of their own children."

He was right. Violence in schools, broken families, hungry children right here in our town, we didn't have to go far to find these things. I felt as though I was going to be sick. "So what do we do now?"

Thor stood, and all but Zeus and Apollo followed suit. "I have things I must attend to." He nodded toward his seated men. "They will inform you of the plan of action."

Krisz stood. "I'm going to put J.J. down first."

I nodded. "Let's get them settled for the night. What time is it?" I asked Mitch.

He looked at his watch and shook his head. "Wow, it's already past ten. OK, I'll get Jamie to bed."

Krisz came back to the table. "They're both out, in pajamas and under the covers."

I looked down at Ally. "Then why aren't you asleep as well?"

She made a face. "Because I had something portent to say."

I laughed. "Im-portant." I gave her a kiss on the top of her head and handed her to Krisz.

While Krisz got Ally through her bedtime routine, I tended to the fire. I turned to find that our 'furniture' had been restored, and without the slightest sound. The exhaustion of the past few hours had caught up with me. Although by now it could have been days, who knew? Mitch had heated up some water on the single burner and held up a selection of teas and cocoa. I pointed to the caramel hot chocolate sachet. Krisz tugged on the chocolate mint one as she came around the table to sit.

Zeus and Apollo joined us at the table. Mitch passed out our cups and turned to offer some to them. "You can have tea, coffee or hot chocolate," he said as he held out a selection of packets. There were dark circles under his eyes and he was overdue for a shave. He looked the way I felt.

"Thank you," Apollo said as he accepted a steaming cup from Mitch. He took a moment to savor his drink.

Sipping from my cup as I looked around the room, I was overcome by a wave of sadness. Yes, I wanted to see my parents, but even more, I wanted to keep in contact with my new family.

Krisz had propped her elbows on the table and was resting her forehead against the cup she held in her hands. "I don't mean to be rude or anything, but I really need some sleep. Can we get on with it?"

Lowering his empty cup to the table, Apollo began to explain. "First of all, your world leaders are in little position to resist. We will impose a reformation of government and abolish currency. You will either care for one another as well as your planet, or we will resume consuming it."

I was startled by his statement. I could not imaginee how they were going to bring that about.

"You do not have to know the details. Suffice it to say that everyone has the right to food, shelter and education. Every member is expected to contribute according to their abilities." He studied my face.

"But how's that supposed to work?" I was confused. No money? I caught a look of bewilderment on Krisztina's face.

"You will come to understand in time." Zeus cut in. "Try to imagine every person being allowed to study what they like, what they are good at, and it no longer being a question of money or prestige."

Apollo leaned forward. "This will also apply to jobs. People will be able to do the job they love because they love it. The single mother who works as a store clerk will no longer have to put in sixty hours a week to try and feed her children."

I began to wonder just how long they'd been thinking about all this if a plan so intricate was already in place. I tried to imagine such a thing. "Where did this idea, this project come from?"

A look of sorrow crossed both Zeus and Apollo's face at the same time. Zeus answered, his words carefully chosen. "This is how it was for us for so very long ago." He shot a glance at Apollo. "Until our sun grew into a red giant and our planet was destroyed."

"There are only a few hundred of us left," Apollo said grimly. "Only those who were out on patrol when the star shifted survived. Along with a training expedition consisting of 37 females and fifty males all under the age of reproduction, we will not be able to continue increasing our population for another few years." He became silent, seemingly lost in thought.

"We have become scavengers, feeding off of other planets simply to survive," Zeus added.

"Will you settle here?" I asked.

Apollo shrugged. "It is still undecided. Your race can be quite barbaric, and we had left violence behind us a long time ago."

"But you destroyed our city!" Mitch interjected. "Several cities."

They both nodded.

"But no one was hurt, right?" I asked.

"As a direct result of our intervention, no," Zeus answered.

I chewed on my bottom lip, trying to figure out what would happen next. In response to my silent question Apollo answered. "You can remain here, together, while the new community is built. The parcel of land is big enough to accommodate the families that had been relocated. Your families can settle around the shelter in temporary homes until their permanent dwellings have been built."

I saw the relief I felt reflected in Krisz's face. I didn't want to lose my family either. A thought crossed my mind. "And you think the government is just going to let you impose all these changes?"

"They will have no choice but to comply," Zeus answered. "We have effectively neutralized all of your weapons." He glanced at Apollo. "We did not expect them to comply willingly. Time will tell."

Six Months Later

I stood at the door of the shelter and looked around. Many of the temporary, mobile homes would no longer be needed. Construction had finally been completed on the latest series of town houses and cottages, and our new town center had come to life with everyone chipping in. No one had been paid for their work or services which had gone over surprisingly well. Teaching people not to hoard food had been a challenge, though. They'd had a hard time understanding that everyone was entitled to eat, and that no one would go without. Wasting was frowned upon, and just plain not tolerated.

The community was made up of people who chose to be part of the new city. They embraced this new way of thinking, and new way of life, where everyone contributed to the general well-being of everyone else. Mom had set up a medical clinic and Dad headed the rebuild. It was nice to have them on *my* project this time. I smiled to myself as I thought of our reunion. Dad had said he was proud of me, and impressed as he visited our shelter. Mom had said she loved me. Nothing could replace what that meant to me.

"Hey!" Krisztina called out as she passed by, surrounded by a group of children. I smiled. Teaching had also been changed to include more of a hands-on approach. Ally and J.J. ran up to me and each hugged a leg. "Come on back you two," Krisz called out to them.

I watched as they scurried back to the group, waving. I had been worried about losing sight of our survival group for nothing. We lived close enough to one another that not a day went by where our paths didn't cross at least once, and I wouldn't have it any other way. Our age didn't keep us from participating in the town we'd built. Everyone had a role to play.

Apollo pulled up in the Jeep we had taken so long ago and Mitch stuck his head out the passenger side window. "Let's get a move on! We're visiting the new site today."

I shook my head. This whole planetary restructuring sure made things strange. Children had a say in their future and well-being. Thor had spread his people around the world, and being telepathic helped avert messy situations. Once the governments realized, or maybe accepted, that the *Greek Gods* were there to help, not take over, tension fell and progress was made.

"Hey," I called back to Mitch. "It's my turn to ride up front."

Jamie poked his head out of the back seat. "But I don't want to sit with him," he whined. "I wanted to sit with you."

I smiled. How could I resist that?

About the Author

Over the years I have worked as a nurse, a school teacher, a martial arts instructor, baseball, figure-skating and gymnastics coach as well as an artist, selling my paintings in an art gallery. I have been part of an orchestra, flown planes and gone on wilderness hikes. I am an officer in the Canadian Forces, and though I have taught on different military bases, for now I work primarily with cadets. Writing full time is my next goal.

Connect with Debbie

WEBSITE: http://welcometomywritingworld.weebly.com/
BLOG: http://amethysteyesauthor.blogspot.ca/
TWITTER: https://twitter.com/amethysteyes01

Books by Debbie Brown

Amethyst Eyes

Amethyst Eyes: The Legend Comes to Life

Rebirth

Emma… to Begin Again

www.ingramcontent.com/pod-product-compliance
Lightning Source LLC
Chambersburg PA
CBHW070326130626
46556CB00007B/2746